THE ROAD TO NOEWARE

WOVEN BRANCHES

A SOUTHERN SERIAL

G.L. YANCY

For Rita Faye Yancy, may she rest in peace.

The Road to Noeware
Copyright © 2023 by G.L. Yancy

Editing:
Cover Design by: AuthorTree
Interior Book Formatting: AuthorTree

All rights reserved under the International and Pan-American Copyright Conventions. No part of this book may be reproduced or transmitted in any form or by any means, electronic or mechanical, including photocopying, recording, or by any information storage and retrieval system, without permission in writing from the publisher.

This is a work of fiction. Names, places, characters and incidents are either the product of the author's imagination or are used fictitiously, and any resemblance to any actual persons, living or dead, organizations, events or locales is entirely coincidental.

Warning: the unauthorized reproduction or distribution of this copyrighted work is illegal. Criminal copyright infringement, including infringement without monetary gain, is investigated by the FBI and is punishable by up to 5 years in prison and a fine of $250,000.

PROLOGUE

Friday Night, September 26

Thunder clapped on the sultry late September evening in South Georgia. A promise to break the seemingly never-ending drought, or just another tease? For two months, storms had come close enough to taste, but taken their rain elsewhere, leaving only unbearable humidity in their wake. Would the eighth time be a charm? Only time would tell. "Rain already, for the love of God," he thought as he proceeded slowly down a mostly deserted Main Street on what seemed like the darkest night of the year thus far. Summer's sizzle was slowly giving way to that in-between season particular to the south. Autumn's cooler weather would be coming soon enough, but not without some serious resistance.

It was soccer season for the children who participated in the recreational league, and his son had an early match in the morning. Little chance of his own actual attendance at the game at this point, his gut groaned with sickness at the thought of his ex-wife's reaction to his job coming before his children, *again*. Afterall, situations such as this were the precise reason that his divorce seemed inevitable from the very beginning of his later in life marriage. A man can be married to a woman, or he can be married to his work, but a polygamist relationship with both is rarely possible.

The downtown night was quiet, too quiet for a late Friday, early Saturday. One would almost describe the evening as peaceful, if he were unaware of the current events. The city was hardly a party haven, but there were a few bars on the edge of town that would normally provide activity well into the morning hours. On this night, there was no such activity. As he drew closer to the scene, he could see the flashing lights, like a 1970s mirrorball in a disco reflecting off the aged brick of the fine hotel. Wide-eyed guests stared in confusion and disbelief as they lined the sidewalk in the near early morning hour. Some folks were nervously smoking cigarettes while debating the evening's events with strangers and family members alike. Others were pacing with an impatient need for sleep before early morning meetings, departures from town or shopping adventures in not so nearby places. Nearly all the bystanders were wearing various forms of sleepwear, some covered with robes, many not, as they had fled their rooms in haste at the behest of hotel security, other staff members or local law enforcement. This was an all-hands-on-deck type of situation.

He parked the car in a loading zone, with his own lights spinning like a beacon for the ones who had arrived before. Several uneasy passersby approached him with bewilderment as he slowly maneuvered from behind his steering wheel. Shutting his vehicle door with a loud slam that seemed to announce his command of the situation that he had yet to observe, he asked for everyone to remain calm, though he knew his words were futile before they left his tongue. A thin layer of sweat immediately coated his skin as he quickly left the cool comfort of his air-conditioned car and stepped into the thick night air. No sooner had he done so than the nearer elements of the crowd drew toward him like iron shavings following a magnet. Their questions tripped and fell over one another and kept any of them from clearly reaching his ears. He raised his voice to a louder pitch and repeated his request for calm. Again, to no avail.

His outfit seemed highly inappropriate for the call that he was responding to, but he, like the hotel guests and staff, wasn't exactly given much warning. Wearing jeans, loafers and a teal and black flannel shirt, his appearance was much more L.L. Bean, than chief of police. Yet, chief of police he was, and had been for the past five years. He thought grimly about the folks that would surely make what hay they could out of his lack of formality. The city's first African American chief of police was held to a higher standard than his predecessors, and a dress uniform would have been much more appropriate for the circumstances, but tonight was a unique situation. Fortunately, he thought most would forgive the breach in protocol; the others would have to live with it. Thunder boomed and lightning flashed, as everyone gasped and averted their eyes from nature's strobe light. "Damn tease," he muttered under his breath while looking up into the pitch night sky.

Chief Ernie Thomas nodded to the uniformed officer working impromptu crowd control just outside the entrance to the Grand Hotel.

"Chief, Detective Abernathy is waiting for you in the lobby," he said.

"Thanks Jones, maybe we should have someone on the hotel staff work on finding these fine people a place to lay their heads for the night. Is Gail Wilson here somewhere?"

"If she is here Chief, I sure haven't seen her, but Claire Montgomery is just inside."

"Oh Christ! Thanks for the warning."

Claire Montgomery had been the general manager of the Grand Hotel for as long as most folks in town could remember. Sister to the county's most senior commissioner, and a descendant of one of the area's founding fathers, she pulled a lot of weight in town politics. Much more than a glorified hotel concierge, Claire was the Grande dame of the city's business district, and she would let no one forget it. With an aura of strength, mixed with a certain southern gentility, she was the perfect hostess to represent the city's biggest tourist destination. She was also less human, and more machine when it came to business matters — sort of a forever working android in haute couture.

"Ernie, it's about time you got here," she said as she held the door open for the chief. Claire, as usual was perfectly coiffed, not a bottled blonde hair out of place, and dressed impeccably in a burgundy Armani suit.

"Now Claire, without the help of teleportation, I couldn't have gotten here much faster."

"This is an unmitigated public relations disaster, Chief. I want this situation under control *yesterday*."

"Your warmth and concern for the victim are noted Claire, I'll see what I can do about cleaning up your little inconvenience as fast as I can," the chief responded sarcastically, while rolling his eyes. "Now, are we doing anything about a change of accommodations for your guests?"

"Obviously, I wasn't going to wait on your word to start the hotel's emergency protocols; I might have been waiting all night. Daisy is on the phone now firming up arrangements with other establishments."

"Daisy? I would have thought your niece, being the front desk manager, would have been assigned that task."

"While I appreciate your acknowledgement of the hotel's chain of command, you would do better to concentrate on your job, Ernie. I will worry about the guests at my hotel," she said while wondering exactly why in the hell her usually very conscientious niece Gail wasn't answering her phone. The chief was correct, this is a job that Gail should be doing. "Chief Thomas, there wasn't a guest assigned to the room where the situation at hand took place, since it was on the fourth floor. As you no doubt recall, the entire fourth floor has been closed for renovation for the past six months."

"So, if there wasn't a guest assigned to that room, what exactly are we dealing with here?" the chief asked; he wasn't expecting an answer. He hadn't finished his sentence before Claire had turned to issue a crisp set of instructions to what appeared to be an assistant. Ernie kept his eyes on her for a beat as she walked off, and by the time he'd turned back to face the lobby, a tall brooding man was standing before him.

"Ah, Chief Thomas," Detective Luke Abernathy said by way of greeting, as the men firmly shook hands and shared a concerned look undetectable to an outside observer. Detective Abernathy was wearing a rather ordinary gray suit, but it was covered optimistically in an oversized tan trench coat built for rain. His tie had been loosened and his top button disengaged, in a futile attempt to cool off just a bit.

"Why don't you tell me what we've got on the way upstairs, Luke, and take that damn coat off, you're giving me sympathy sweats," Chief Thomas said as the men headed towards a flight of stairs.

"Sorry Chief, I haven't had a moment since I walked in the door. The victim is female, appears to be in her mid-40s, tall, with a large frame. She's a big woman, in stature I mean, not at all obese."

"Burglary?" asked the chief in response to the quick briefing.

"Honestly Ernie, it could be a burglary; we haven't found her purse yet. But most burglars don't stick around long enough to stab their victims over 20 times."

"Holy Shit," a shocked Chief Thomas replied. "Sounds like there was some serious anger behind that blade."

"You're not kidding," Abernathy agreed. "This sort of thing may happen in Atlanta or Augusta, but I have never seen anything like it here."

"Let's keep the details under wraps until we know more, Luke. The last thing we need is for the news media to pick this up and run rampant with speculation. Have someone call Carl

Washington over at the Journal. Let him know that we will issue a statement, and he is not to print anything outside of that statement until he receives word from us. Let's just stick to 'no comment', with the reporters from out of town. There is never a good time for something like this to happen, but there sure couldn't be a worse time, this hotel is full of media types."

"You got it Chief," Detective Abernathy replied as he dropped his boss off at the door of the crime scene and shifted over to a quiet corner to call Carl Washington, the editor of the county's only newspaper.

Bright yellow tape imprinted with the words "Crime Scene" blocked the entrance to Room 412. Besides ribbon cutting ceremonies to mark the opening of new businesses, this town wasn't used to bunting like this draped so provocatively across a doorway. Bending carefully under the tape, as he entered the room, Ernie Thomas was painfully reminded that he wasn't a young man anymore. Clutching lightly at his low back, it took him a few seconds to regain a standing position. Once his proper posture was restored, he got his first look at the hotel room.

Upon an initial glance, the area near the hotel room door appeared to be staged for a romantic interlude. Crimson colored rose petals were scattered in a haphazard trail across the floor for a few feet. The red from the petals was so dark against emerald green and gold carpeting, that they were nearly black. It was only due to the metallic smell perfuming the air, and the knowledge that a stabbing had occurred, that one realized these weren't natural adornments from a flower at all, but large drops of blood from an initial wound. A few feet further into the room, the situation became crystal clear.

Blood spatter rested artistically across the light beige walls, as if it was a work of modern abstract art in an urban museum, or some sort of macabre Rorschach test. That wasn't the extent of the horrific decor, as blood and gray matter reached high onto the matte white ceiling as well, allowing a small glimpse into the sheer violence of this evening's occurrence. This was a scene one would expect to read about in a crime novel, not witness in the most upscale hotel in a small southern town.

The body of the female victim was lying ungracefully on its side, between two double beds, like a traveler's heavy duffle bag thrown on the floor in exhaustion. She was wearing a thick white Grand Hotel terrycloth robe, as if she was freshly showered, or preparing to turn in for the night. The robe now resembled more of an unimaginative two-toned tie dye dress, as blood soaked through its material. Detective Abernathy had not exaggerated the woman's build, her legs seemed to go on forever.

Her position, lying on her left side, gave a limited view of her wounds. Obvious were the slashes to her palms, which were clearly defensive in nature, and the many gashes to her face, head, neck and chest, which probably took place as she lay supine on the floor. In this condition, the chief wasn't sure that even a close relative would be able to identify this woman beyond a reasonable doubt. Brutality like this implied passion or hate — or both.

It is important for one not to lose perspective in instances such as this, Ernie Thomas thought to himself. The body on the hotel room floor is not simply a victim, a corpse, a fatality. Though a homicide scene is looked at in both a clinical and analytical way, the fact of the matter is, this is someone's daughter, wife or mother. It is the level of humanity that exists within a detective that separates the good from the great — the ability to empathize with a family's loss. Though he hasn't been simply a detective for years, Ernie Thomas still thought like one. He must think like one. There was someone out there who cared for, probably very deeply, the person whose life was cut short in this room. The person who would never again come home from work to prepare dinner. The person who would not be there to tuck her children into their beds at night. The person who was now rendered incapable of making love to her soulmate. This is a loss that is deep and personal for someone, or, more than likely, many people. This crime didn't have to be solved just for the family and friends of the victim, though they were first and foremost, Chief Thomas needed it solved for himself, so that he could live with himself, so that when he looked in the mirror each morning, he could respect the man that stared back at him.

"Ladies and gentlemen, I want to know who our victim is, and who had it in for her. Get me some answers pronto, before I am inevitably summoned to the mayor's office tomorrow," the chief of police exclaimed as his cellphone buzzed with the dreaded word "mayor" on the display screen. "Anybody have a Tums?" Ernie Thomas asked as he shook his head, took a deep breath and answered the incoming call that he had hoped wouldn't come for several hours yet.

"We've found a purse," yelled someone from across the room.

Outside the hotel room window, the dark plum colored sky unleashed hell, as the summer's most aggressive thunderstorm made its way through Noeware, Ga.

PART ONE

Tuesday, September 23
Three Days Prior to the Murder

CHAPTER 1
THE ROAD TO NOEWARE

The noxious smell of gas fumes and engine oil she ingested over the last three hours were starting to take a toll. Her slightly blurred vision and light sensitivity suggested that a full-blown migraine was a distinct possibility. Her low back ached from the lack of lumbar support in the bus seat, but the ride would be coming to an end soon. She pulled her khaki jumper dress back down towards her sandals, as she had done countless times while sitting in the uncomfortable teal paisley seat, partly because the cotton material kept riding up, partly because she was fidgeting anxiously anticipating finally reaching her destination. She felt completely drenched in perspiration from head to toe.

Though she had been glancing out the window at the passing scenery, for countless hours, her focus had mostly been on a tiny cobweb spider weaving a new home in the space between the two seats in front of her. She was fascinated by the determination of the arachnid, who she knew probably completed this same mundane task every day. She could certainly relate to the monotony. She stretched her neck from side to side and tried to direct her attention to her destination.

Noeware, Georgia is the county seat of Tennyson County, located in the southwest quadrant of the Peach State. Allison had completed as much research on the place as possible, before hitting the road. Noeware's population rests at around 17,000 people, making it neither a one stop light town, nor anything like its northern cousin, the sprawling state capitol of Atlanta, where Allison Edwards made her home. Tennyson County, in many ways, appeared to be a throwback to the Old South, a large Caucasian population, meshed with an even larger minority community, the majority of which is African American. Allison was looking forward to seeing the place in person, rather than just relying on data she had gathered from the internet.

The little spider busied herself spinning her silk around more layers of web, all of which were so fine they could barely be seen with the naked eye. The weaver never rested. She seemed never to tire, as she worked feverishly to finish the job at hand — how Allison knew what this life was like. Day after day, hour after hour, she went through the motions of project completion, never stopping to realize that life was passing her by.

There were several more hours remaining until sunset, as the bus entered Tennyson County. Outside the windows, that were incapable of being opened, though she had tried repeatedly, Allison saw a picturesque rural landscape. Corn and peanut fields surrounded the two-lane road. Poplar, pine and palm trees were visible as well. She would find the eclectic mix of foliage peculiar if it weren't for the knowledge that both the Alabama and the Florida state lines were within a relatively short driving distance. This broad mix of climates lends itself to majestic moss-covered trees, sprawling crop filled acres and alligator sightings in local ponds, or at least that is what the internet told her. Soon enough, she would see for herself.

Another thing that she learned about the area online was that it was best known for two structures, Tennyson General Hospital, a regional trauma center, and the Grand Hotel, which stood at 10 beautifully aged brick stories. The hospital, at an impressive six stories, stood on Main Street near the Grand Hotel, and together they were the tallest buildings in town. The contrast between the two structures couldn't be more pronounced, as the hospital was a gray utilitarian structure, made more basic in the shadow of the hotel's grandeur.

The county's major economic resource, again, according to her internet research, is agriculture. Corn, tobacco, peanuts and pecans are all harvested daily from the farms of Tennyson County, loaded onto a train, with a still-in-service steam engine and delivered to the factories on the other side of town. The train makes a loop around the county, and only caters to the county, accomplishing tasks that are carried out by tractor trailer trucks in most places. It is one of the features that make this spot on the map quirky and unique. Very reminiscent of locomotive rides one might find at countless theme parks across the country.

The lack of traffic on the highway into town was astonishing to Allison, as one might encounter a traffic jam in Atlanta just making a quick run to a convenience store. Allison couldn't help but wonder what life must be like in a town with so few inhabitants. She jumped slightly as the bus brakes squealed, as if they were announcing the arrival of the passengers to town. "City of Noeware, Georgia, Ruth Blakely, Mayor", read a sign by the road positioned perfectly in a bed of yellow and rust colored chrysanthemums. "You go, sister," Allison mumbled to herself with a smile at the thought of a female mayor, presiding over a small town in the deep South. The bus seemed to huff, as if its nonexistent lungs were giving out from the long journey.

Looking back at her web constructing friend, she wondered if spiders had community. Was there a hierarchy within their species? Perhaps this busy lady in front of her was the governor of some spider state, the mayor of a city, or just another cog in a corporate machine — like Allison. She laughed to herself, realizing that her silly thoughts were bordering on delirium. Jeez, she had been on this bus for too long.

The scenery along the highway changed drastically as the drive continued. Fields and trees faded from sight, as weathered, and in some cases dilapidated, buildings came into view. Allison noted that they were no longer traveling on the stretch of road marked "Scenic Highway", as the name had changed to "E. Grey Street" once the city limits were reached. Again, the bus brakes moaned, as the trip's destination was reached.

Taking a final look at the spider, while her fellow passengers stood up from their uncomfortable seats, Allison had to admit that the work she had witnessed was impressive. What had simply been empty space a few hours ago, was now filled with a beautiful lacy curtain. So delicate was the web, yet strong enough to support both the spider and her prey. What pride she must take in her creation.

Allison jumped suddenly, as a clenched fist smashed the web, and with it the spider, right before her eyes. She looked up to see a man in a baseball cap, with a Georgia Bulldogs insignia displayed on the front, looking back down at her. "Damn bugs," he said, wiping the mess off his fist onto his faded blue jeans. He then continued toward the exit door; a backpack strapped over one shoulder. Allison watched him leave the bus, still shocked by the realization that a few seconds ago, this spider was full of life and working, and now she was dead, as if she had never existed at all.

ALLISON GROANED WITH RELIEF, AS SHE DISEMBARKED from the tubular prison she had been sentenced to for the better part of the day and made her way through the flurry of activity towards the bus's mid-section. She patiently waited for the driver to unload the scarcely packed storage compartment, so that she could identify her suitcase. Allison was not what one would call a seasoned traveler. In fact, the endless hours that she spent managing a corporately owned coffee house ensured that she was not well traveled at all. Vacation days were few and far between, usually reserved for responsibilities such as jury duty or annual car maintenance. This trip was an anomaly, made possible only by the grant that she received from the Noeware Journal newspaper to write a human-interest story about its town.

Allison Edwards and her partner Jessica Walters were minding their own business, muddling through their boring, but relatively happy existence, when a letter arrived out of the blue. Allison, who attends virtual journalism classes online at Georgia State University, had apparently garnered the attention of a small-town daily newspaper in South Georgia for a story she had written about Anniston, a tiny town located in eastern Alabama. The Anniston story had been submitted to the *Birmingham Gazette* by her Feature Writing professor, for consideration in a series that was running on rural revitalization. To her surprise and delight, Allison's story was well received, accepted and made its way into the highly circulated paper. It was one of Allison's proudest moments. Jessica, who works as a compliance official with the Atlanta based Centers for Disease Control, had been over the moon for her "better half." She admired Allison's creativity, and in contrast to her own job, which could be a bureaucratic nightmare, Jessica enjoyed living vicariously through the excitement of Allison's future career.

To the women, the decision was an absolute no brainer, when the letter arrived with the offer of a modest financial grant, substantial to this middle-class household, that offered the opportunity for a little adventure in exchange for Allison writing the feature story. The only brief hesitation came from the realization that Jessica would be unable to accompany Allison to Noeware, Georgia (wherever the hell that was), because she had pressing deadlines at the office. However, this uncertainty was quickly resolved when the ladies acknowledged what a huge opportunity had been dropped into their laps, and that Allison really wouldn't be away for more than a week or so. Not to mention, nearly five days a week, Jessica was in the Indianapolis area for work. She traveled constantly in her position with the CDC. She and Allison saw each other rarely on weekdays anyway.

With the decision made, the offer was accepted via a phone call to the editor in chief of the *Noeware Journal*, a Mr. Carl Washington, who could not have been more kind and encouraging. Allison made arrangements to take a few weeks of her earned vacation time that she had built up at work, turned her store, located in the village near Emory University in Atlanta, over to her assistant manager, and bought a bus ticket. Though she owned a decent car, Jessica thought better of Allison risking a flat tire or engine breakdown alone on a secluded country road on the way to South Georgia. Allison couldn't have agreed more.

Now, here she was, suitcase in hand, walking towards the exit of the dingy bus terminal, and into a new adventure. As she passed a concrete column located near the door, she saw a small graffiti message scrawled out with a black sharpie:

WELCOME TO NOWHERE…
WHY ARE YOU HERE!

"Good question," Allison thought to herself with a smirk and a shrug, "guess we'll soon find out."

CHAPTER 2
NOEWARE, GA

Allison stopped briefly at a bench just outside of the bus terminal. Although it was approaching dinnertime, the sun's rays were still relentless. The afternoon heat was scorching, and it showed no signs of letting up. She sat down for a second, collecting her thoughts and taking in her surroundings. The town, what she could see of it from here anyway, was charming. Across the street, she could see the Grand Hotel, where she had reserved a room for the next several days. Though the building would hardly be noticed back home in Atlanta, it was nothing short of magnificent in this setting. Across the street from the hotel was a retro diner called "Middle of Noeware". Clever. It was built in the 1950s style, with lots of chrome and windows. The eatery looked like it belonged on a movie set, and Allison knew instantly where she would be having breakfast in the morning. She was already in love with the town's quaintness. She could get used to a slower pace. In the distance, the whistle from a steam engine could be heard.

A high-pitched squeaking sound caught her attention from the end of the block. Glancing in that general direction, she noticed what appeared to be a portly older woman, frizzy gray hair pulled back in a disheveled bun, pulling a small luggage cart that held a single suitcase. The woman had a face that could have belonged to an accident victim, sagging on the left side as if she had nerve damage and permanently inflamed on the right, as if she had a boil or a cyst on her rosy cheek. "Interesting," she whispered to herself, as she could not place the woman's face among the few bus passengers that she had traveled with from the city. Yet, the woman had to have been in the bus terminal, why else would she be pulling a suitcase?

Wearing ill-fitting brown slacks, and a button-down navy blouse that was untucked at the waist, the woman appeared to be confused. "Good evening, Miss Willa," "Hot out tonight, Miss Willa," "Getting by okay, Miss Willa?", passersby said by way of greeting her. She was obviously a fixture in this town, and this was exactly the type of local flavor that Allison had hoped to experience while here. As the woman moved down the sidewalk, and closer to where Allison sat on the bench, she noticed that there was something in the woman's hand. It appeared to be a book of some sort. It was easier to see, as the woman, obviously exhausted from the heat and her walk, sat in the empty space next to Allison on the bench. Seated, the woman seemed closer to Allison in height, though standing, she appeared to be a good foot slighter.

"Miss Willa, I presume," Allison asked as the woman

breathed an extended exhale and wiped her sweat-beaded brow with the sleeve of her blouse.

"Are you, my little girl?" the old woman asked in astonishment at being recognized by a stranger.

"Oh no, I'm sorry," Allison responded, feeling badly that she had added to the woman's obvious confusion.

"Bahahahahaha," the woman laughed abruptly, causing Allison to flush with embarrassment. "Don't you think I'd know my own child, girl? I was just messing with ya."

"Oh." Allison said in response, as she giggled a little uncomfortably. "Since I already know your name, I think it's fair to give you mine. I'm Allison Edwards."

"They call me Willa. I don't know why, but that's what they call me."

"I'm very honored to meet you, Willa. Are you from Noeware?"

"Everybody is from somewhere girl, for me that somewhere is Noeware. Yes, is what I am tryin' to say."

Allison was absolutely enchanted by this woman. She was like a character in a storybook. Though her words were simple, there was a sense of wisdom behind them. She had eyes that contained a child's innocence, but a face that looked haggard and defeated. Allison was very interested in knowing the woman's story, and she knew for sure that there was a story there.

"Were you on the bus that just arrived?" Allison asked the woman, eager to keep the conversation's flow going.

"Oh no girl, I travel by train. I am what you call a train enthusiast."

"The train here in town? But I thought that the train only

serviced the county. Surely you don't mean that you need luggage to travel around here by train?" Allison said, but instantly regretted the words, as she realized that Willa was potentially homeless. The very last thing that Allison wanted was to make the woman feel as if she was being looked down on. Allison was no stranger to the homeless community back in Atlanta. They could detect her bleeding heart from miles away, and she was happy to provide safe companionship for them.

Willa's eyes glassed over, and her look became distant, as she stared deeply into nothingness. She remained in this state for more than a few long seconds, though it felt like hours to Allison. The old woman appeared to be repeating a single word over and over, but Allison was unable to make it out. With a sudden jerk of her head, Willa made eye contact with Allison again, produced a picture from between the tattered pages of the Bible in her hand and asked, "Have you seen my little girl?" Allison's eyes welled up with tears, and her stomach turned somersaults as she looked at the picture. It appeared to have been taken in the early '70s or thereabout, it was in color, but that kind of faded early color. The girl in the photograph was beautiful. She had gorgeous dark hair, she was slim, smiling, wearing a denim jumpsuit. She appeared to be about three years of age. Allison had no idea if the woman was really missing a daughter, but she knew for sure that Willa believed that she was.

"She's lovely," Allison responded honestly, "but, I am afraid that I haven't seen her."

Willa made no attempt to respond. She went back into what appeared to be a trance. Allison slowly stood from the bench, wiping the tears that had formed in her eyes with her thumb, and started to make her way towards the Grand Hotel. She was confident that she would run into Miss Willa again during her stay in Noeware. The woman's situation made her sad, but right now she just wanted to check into her room and call Jess.

CHAPTER 3
NOEWARE, GA, GRAND HOTEL

The large glass and brass doors of the Grand Hotel were heavy as Allison maneuvered through them while trying not to drop her suitcase. The South Georgia heat was weighing heavily on her, as it was a good ten degrees hotter here than was normal back home. There was no doorman as she had been accustomed to seeing in larger Atlanta hotels. The door shut softly on her foot as she tried to get through unscathed. She just laughed and shook her head as she collected herself and looked around to be sure that no one else had been witness to her clumsiness. The cool climate-controlled air felt heavenly as it blasted every pore of Allison's skin. She was instantly glad that Jess had talked her into staying at the Grand. "The place is one of the city's biggest attractions, of course you'll be staying there," Jess had said, totally discounting Allison's arguments about the cost.

She made her way to the large ornate oak front desk, where she was able to step right up, as the guest before her had just finished conducting business. "Welcome to the Grand Hotel," an attractive young Asian woman with an eye patch said by way of greeting her, "I'll be right with you, just as soon as I can figure out why my screen has gone blank." The look of utter confusion on her face made Allison smile with empathy, thinking of her own learning curve when dealing with new technology back at the coffee shop. Computers were not exactly Allison's best friends.

"Daisy, I'll be happy to help our guest, if you are ready to clock out for the evening, I know it has been a long day," a pleasant middle-aged woman in a navy floral dress said, obviously attempting to rescue her young employee in a rather nonchalant way. She had a pencil tucked behind her left ear, which seemed a perfect complement to her disheveled blonde hair. Her nametag, hanging crookedly above her right breast read, "Gail Wilson, Front Desk Manager".

"Now, Ms. ...", she questioned, while directing her kind eyes toward Allison.

"Edwards, um Allison Edwards," she replied, not used to the procedure of checking into a finer establishment. "I should have a reservation. I think we made it a while ago."

"Oh, it's a pleasure to meet you Ms. Edwards. Let's find that reservation for you," Gail Wilson said as she pulled up the reservation screen that had been accidentally minimized by the other young desk agent. "You'll have to excuse my assistant Daisy. We've been very short staffed lately. I am afraid that she is a bit scattered when well rested, so this week has been even more of a strain."

"Think nothing of it," Allison replied, "I manage a store in Atlanta and haven't been fully staffed for several years now."

"That seems the way of the business world these days, doesn't it, Ms. Edwards," Gail responded while pulling out a magnetic key card. "Will Ms. Walters still be joining you on your stay with us?"

"Oh no, I'm here alone to write a story on your town for the newspaper, we must have used Jess's credit card to reserve the room. I'm sorry, is that going to be a problem?"

"No problem at all," Gail Wilson reassured her, "you are all squared away. Here's your key. I hope you enjoy your stay with us."

Allison thanked the front desk manager for her help and hobbled over to the elevator, dodging several people wearing press credentials. She had to admit that Jess had been right, she packed way too heavily for a weeklong trip. The elevator door opened, Allison entered, and as the door closed, she couldn't help but notice that Gail Wilson's focus seemed to still be on her.

Once the front desk was completely clear of guests, Gail slid out her cellphone and pulled up her contacts. She looked around quickly to be sure that she wasn't overheard.

"Gail, what is it? I'm in the middle of making my evening rounds," Dr. Meg Givens asked her sister as she hurriedly answered her call.

"I'm just letting you know that she just checked in."

As the elevator ascended, Allison studied her reflection in the metal door. "Jesus, Allison, I see a long hot shower in your very near future," she mused. The elevator opened with a ding, and Allison stepped out looking around the walls for a directional sign. She followed the taupe wallpapered hallway until she found her room. Her magnetic key card worked, after the second try, as she had inadvertently slid it into its slot backwards. "I really am exhausted," she laughed to herself as she entered the room.

Lifting the weight of her suitcase, she placed it on the perfectly made bed and sat down beside it. A quick glance around was all it took to prove to her that she and Jess had made the right decision, if she was going to stay for a week in a little town where she knew no one, she might as well pamper herself a little. The room even had a desk in the corner that was more than adequate for Allison to use for her work.

She jumped suddenly, as she was startled by the Indigo Girls song "Power of Two" blaring from her pocket, the ringtone assigned to Jess in her phone. Laughing at herself, she answered quickly, "Jess, you are not going to believe this place. This is the nicest hotel room that I have ever been in. I just got here, after the longest bus ride of my life. The countryside was amazing. Then we arrived at the bus station, which was a little sketchy, and I met the most interesting lady."

"Whoa, slow down tiger," Jess's laughing voice replied through the phone, "take a breath before you hyperventilate."

"I'm sorry," Allison replied, "I guess that I am just having a hard time believing that I am really here, on a paid grant, to write a story."

"Well, believe it, Lois Lane, you're an honest to goodness paid journalist now."

Allison giggled at the tease. "There was a little confusion at the front desk, because we used your credit card to reserve the room, but it wasn't a problem that I am staying alone."

"I miss you already," Jess replied distracted by other thoughts, "what are you wearing, sexy?"

Allison laid back on the bed, as the topic of conversation became more intimate. She was suddenly aware that she felt closer to Jess at this moment than she did when they were hundreds of miles closer to one another.

ALLISON WOKE FROM A MUCH-NEEDED NAP AFTER A rather passionate conversation with her partner. She pulled herself off the still made bed, removed her clothes, and headed to the bathroom for a shower. Turning the knobs and holding a hand in the stream to check for temperature, she was aware of how dark the room had gotten. She was also keenly aware of how hungry she was. Perhaps her migraine was brought on by skipping lunch.

The hypnotic sound of the running water took Allison back to her apartment in Atlanta's Old Fourth Ward, where she remembered Jess booking her room at the Grand Hotel. She gasped for two reasons. First, because the water had suddenly gotten too hot and mildly scalded her hand. Second, she remembered for sure that Jess had asked her to retrieve her own credit card to pay the deposit, as Jess had misplaced her card and had to cancel it. How then, Allison wondered, had the hotel had Jess's name?

NEWLY CLEAN, IF NOT EXACTLY REFRESHED BY THE shower, Allison dressed to go out and find some dinner. First, though not much of a drinker, Allison took advantage of the mini bar by having whiskey and diet coke. She was a little confused and unsettled by the room deposit realization, not to mention still suffering from a migraine. The drink should help. She took a few sips, then added more whiskey. A few minutes later, after downing the drink far too quickly, she grabbed her purse and headed for the door. Now, it was definitely time for food.

Allison passed through the lobby quickly, noting that even at this later hour, there were still many members of the press loitering about. She understood that the Grand Hotel would be the accommodation of choice for out-of-town reporters, she just couldn't figure out why so many were here.

Walking outside, she instantly felt the weight of the heavy air. A bout of nausea hit her, as the oppressive heat played havoc with her mostly empty stomach. Well, empty other than the cocktail she had upstairs. She suppressed the urge to be sick and started walking down the mostly deserted sidewalk in the direction of the diner she had seen earlier in the day.

Crossing the street, Allison had the distinct feeling of

being watched. Not just watched, followed. While she didn't see anyone in the darkness that surrounded her, she couldn't shake the feeling. Attempting to stay securely in the rays of the streetlight glow, she continued and listened. Being aware of her surroundings came naturally to Allison, as it did to most people living in big cities, but this wasn't the big city. She was being paranoid and silly, she decided. She had also passed the diner. Another sharp feeling of nausea hit her, or was it panic, as she heard footsteps closing in behind her. Yes, she most definitely heard footsteps. Suddenly, she felt extremely unsafe, she was absolutely not just being silly. Her head was swimming as she grabbed the first door handle she came to. She slung the heavy door open and was instantly consumed by pulsating club music, heat, and the ripe smell of sweat. She ran in, almost tripping over a petite orange tabby cat heading out the door. Trying to regain her balance, she walked straight into an extraordinarily tall woman in a red sequined gown. The last thing Allison saw before passing out was the face of — Patti LaBelle?

PART TWO

Wednesday, September 24
Two Days Prior to the Murder

CHAPTER 4
NOEWARE, GA, THE DINER

Dishes were clanging, coffee was steaming, and voices were loud in the Middle of Noeware Diner. "Billy, this omelet won't carry itself to table three," Ned Wilson yelled from the open kitchen. The bell on the glass front door announced the arrival of Allison Edwards, as she made her way across the black and white tiled floor to the counter in hopes of ordering some breakfast. Sitting on a red vinyl stool beside a distinguished gentleman in a police uniform, she looked up in astonishment.

"Well, girl, honey, I wondered if we'd have the pleasure of your company this morning," Billy Washington beamed from the other side of the counter. He set a fresh cup of coffee in front of her while she stared into his face. "This coffee should help bring you back to life. You look just like that Laura on *General Hospital* when she was coming out of her amnesia."

"Lord, don't get him started," Ned Wilson interrupted, yelling over the noise of his patrons, "yesterday a lady named

Opal was in here, and he went on for 20 minutes about *The Young and the Restless*."

Appalled, Billy replied, "Ned, that was *All My Children*. If you are going to make fun of me, at least reference the right show."

Allison, in her confusion, took a large sip of coffee, "I thought I had the strangest dream last night, and you were there. You were there, too," she exclaimed in the direction of Ned in the kitchen.

"Whoa, slow down there, Dorothy. This ain't Oz," Billy said with a giggle. "You'll have me ducking to avoid flying monkeys in a minute. Those bitches always gave me nightmares."

"Language," Ned admonished from his spot in front of the flat top grill.

Allison, still in a state of confusion, put two and two together. "Wait, you're Patti LaBelle!"

"Well, I have been called many things in my life girl honey, but THAT is legendary," Billy replied, obviously flattered. "They call me Rona Lisa. You know, after the queen of gossip, Ms. Rona Barrett. Although, that damn virus put a damper on my alter ego's first name, I like to think my act is just as infectious."

Ned came around from the kitchen, realizing that Billy had suddenly gone off into la la land, and hadn't noticed Allison was nursing a near empty coffee mug, having quickly downed the beverage in an obvious need for caffeine.

"Oh, so you identify as …"

Billy interrupted Allison's thought, "Identify?" He reached out to block Ned from pouring Allison's brew. "Ned, this one doesn't appear to need any more coffee, she is WOKE enough." "Identify! Really?"

A muted laugh came from the neighboring stool, as the police officer chimed in, "Billy, leave the lady alone. She's a guest in our town and you should probably explain to her what you've spent half the morning telling me about."

"Ned, I am taking a smoke break. You join me over here in this booth, girl, honey, I'll bring us both some fresh coffee."

"You don't smoke," Ned yelled at the back of Billy's head.

Once Billy joined Allison in the booth, he got down to business. "First off, I am Billy Washington, son of the very same Carl Washington that brought you to our little town. My daddy has been running the *Noeware Journal* for going on 15 years. Now, you would think, girl, honey, that you'd be appreciative of the opportunity that my daddy has given you, but instead you pop backstage last night, during the once-a-year appearance of Rona Lisa and almost ruin my show."

"Oh my gosh," Allison replied red faced, "I was sure that I was being followed by someone. I had no idea what was behind the door I grabbed. I am so sorry. I am very embarrassed".

Billy burst out laughing, ready to let her off the hook. "You are going to have to lighten up, if we are going to be friends, Allison Edwards. About 90 percent of what I say is in jest, the other 10 percent is just bullshit," he said with a wink. "Now, you were followed, you say?"

Suddenly, spinning around on the counter stool to face their booth was the law enforcement officer. "I don't mean to eavesdrop, but I couldn't help but overhear. I want to know more about you being followed, as that little piece of information is in my wheelhouse. However, Billy has neglected to tell you a key bit of the story from last night. He was about to go on stage to raise money for the Tennyson County Arts Alliance when you ran through the door. When you fainted, the other performers in the dressing room took care of you while Billy called Ned over there. Ned came to pick you up and take you back to your hotel room."

"But how did Ned know where I was staying? For that matter, why is it that everyone in this town seems to already know me?" Allison asked genuinely confused.

Billy chimed in, "Here's what you need to know about a tiny town like this, girl, honey, everybody is Kevin Bacon. You know, six degrees from everybody else. Daddy wrote a story for the paper about you being awarded the grant that brought you here. There was a picture of you and everything. You are like a local celebrity. It wasn't much of a guess for Ned to figure you were staying at the Grand Hotel and the manager of the front desk is his ex-wife, Gail Wilson. He called her, she confirmed that you were staying there, she opened the room so that Ned could leave you there safely. Of course, you'll not want to mention that to her aunt, who is the general manager, because she'd probably get in trouble for opening the room."

"Well," Allison said relieved, "that explains a lot."

"What it doesn't explain is this you're being followed business," the police officer said. "Forgive my lack of manners, I'm Chief Ernie Thomas. I'd like you to give me a statement about what happened last night, prior to you entering the club, of course. It is not often that someone in this town suggests they are being followed. Sorry if I sound a little dubious, but are you certain about this?"

"I'm not sure that there is very much to tell, Chief Thomas. I am certainly happy to tell you what I know, but is it possible to do that later? I have a meeting this morning with Mr. Washington at the paper. Although, it doesn't sound like you believe me."

"All I am saying," Chief Thomas continued, "is that you are a girl from the big city, staying in an unfamiliar small town, walking around after dark after drinking. Perhaps, you were just a little spooked by the unfamiliar surroundings."

Great, Allison thought, now the entire town is going to be thinking that she is a paranoid drunk, because a drag queen and a short order cook smelled liquor on her breath. This isn't exactly the first impression that she had hoped to make.

"I'll have you know Chief Thomas, that I am a grown woman, not a *girl*, and I was absolutely not intoxicated last night, at any point. I passed out due to a combination of the heat, which I am not used to, a lack of food, and a severe migraine."

Laughing to himself a little, while clearly enjoying this woman's tenacity, Ernie Thomas responded, "I hear you, Ms. Edwards, and I will look forward to seeing you at the station a little later this afternoon."

As if a paranormal drift of smoke blew through the room, the very air in the diner seemed to change all at once. Not in a literal sense, but in that unusual way that a person's aura can manipulate the space that they inhabit. The diners, while still enjoying their meals, half focused on something happening outside, so Allison glanced in that direction as well. An older woman, with skin the color of dark chocolate was walking by with the assistance of a walker, though she carried herself in a very capable way, in almost an authoritative manner. Everyone that passed the woman made eye contact and spoke, but none of them stopped for conversation. It was as if she exuded an air of unapproachability. She was tall in stature, almost as tall as Allison herself, which was hardly petite. She wore glasses with lenses as thick as cola bottles, and was dressed in a sharp suit, that probably wouldn't be considered necessarily fashionable. Her gray hair was shoulder length and straight, her nails were a clear gloss. She wore very minimal makeup and only basic jewelry. She had a look of complete control, a kind of take-charge type of woman.

"Who is that?" Allison finally asked, though she directed the question to no one in particular.

"Ohhhhhhhh, that's the mayor, girl, honey. Ms. Ruth Blakely. Although everyone calls her 'Ruthless' — not to her face of course. Let's go," Billy said as he grabbed Allison's arm and pulled her out the door.

As Billy bounded out front of the diner, Allison in tow, he inadvertently bumped into a man walking by. "Hey, watch it, queer," the man exclaimed in a loud voice, obviously disgusted by the interaction.

"Why, Cash Waddell, you've been working on your vocabulary words, last week's diss only contained three letters," Billy responded quickly without pausing for further conversation. Allison was in complete disbelief, as blatant homophobia was a rare thing in Atlanta. "Don't look so shocked, girl, honey, there is trash living everywhere, and the Waddell family is about a step or two below your average garbage."

Running up to the mayor, Billy abruptly stopped. "Allison Edwards, I want you to meet Mayor Ruth Blakely."

"William, I know you were taught better manners than to approach a lady on the street and start a conversation without so much as a 'good morning'," the mayor said sternly.

"I'm sorry, Auntie," Billy said as he beamed at the woman he clearly looked up to and loved very much.

As Allison wondered if she had heard Billy correctly when he referred to the mayor as "auntie," the mayor turned to her.

"Welcome to our little town, Ms. Edwards. I trust you'll find your stay informative."

"It's a pleasure to meet you, Mayor Blakely. It would be an honor to sit down with you for an interview at some point."

"Of course," the mayor replied, "my assistant, Tina Hansard, can schedule something for you. Now, if you'll excuse me, I have a pressing matter that I need to attend to first thing."

The mayor continued on her path towards City Hall, leaving Allison to wonder how this woman could have possibly earned the nickname "Ruthless". She seemed very professional and polished to her. A person she could not wait to speak with in relation to her newspaper story.

"Girl, honey, you are in luck. I just happen to know exactly where the *Noeware Journal* is located, and I have a few minutes to escort you over there."

"That's great, thank you so much," Allison replied appreciatively, though she was still starving, having been pulled from the diner before she could order breakfast.

"Now, lesbian, right?" Billy asked while he sized Allison up from top to bottom.

Allison, clearly taken aback by the sudden personal question, replied "I'd say more polyamorous. Meaning …"

"Two Wives," Billy asked in astonishment, pretending to misunderstand what Allison meant.

"Oh, no, not polygamous," Allison quickly corrected.

"Oh, girl, honey, I know what polyamorous is. This may be a backwoods South Georgia town, but we have the Internet. It was installed just after the indoor plumbing," Billy teased as the two of them continued down the sidewalk. "You city folk just have to label everything, don't you?"

"Wait, wasn't it you who just asked about my orientation? Oh, and speaking of labels, do you mind if we discuss this 'girl, honey' thing?" Allison asked cautiously, hoping not to offend her new acquaintance.

"Well, I could see that one coming a mile away. Girl is W.O.K.E.," he yelled with glee, delighted by his new friend's political correctness. Bending down, he scratched the head of the orange tabby cat who had joined them on their walk, "this here's Dewie."

"Oh, hello Dewie, I think we met briefly last night. You sure are a handsome boy, the strong silent type."

"Ha," Billy laughed, "You'll never hear a sound from this one, she's as quiet as a mouse. She is also a beautiful lady. You know, her pronouns are she/her."

Allison laughed at Billy's dig, "okay, that's fair."

As Billy and Allison continued their stroll down the sidewalk, they were unaware of a set of eyes watching their every step. In what could only be described as a mystery novel cliché, the eyes hid behind a copy of the morning edition of the *Noeware Journal*, and sat directly under the brim of a red Georgia Bulldogs cap.

CHAPTER 5
NOEWARE, GA, MAYOR'S OFFICE

Mayor Ruth Blakely picked up the ringing phone on her meticulously organized desk. "Send him in, please," she replied to her assistant, Tina Hansard, as Cash Waddell's arrival was announced.

"Ah, Cash Waddell, I certainly appreciate you taking time out of your less than busy schedule to meet with me this morning," the mayor said as she sat with her hands folded together formally on the desk.

"I have a lot to do today. What did you want to see me for," he asked as he began to take a seat in the finely upholstered chair across from the mayor.

"Uh no, please don't sit. I didn't have this office sanitized for viruses and bacteria, only to allow some fungus to take root on the furniture."

"You …," Cash started to mumble under his breath before Ruth Blakely interrupted him.

"Finish that sentence Mr. Waddell and I will have the

police department raid that rusted out tin can your family calls a home before you can order lunch from the dollar menu at the diner." Ruth arched an eyebrow and sat up just a little straighter in her chair as she looked directly into his eyes, "let's pretend that I am a priest. Is there anything that you'd like to confess?"

"I don't do confession. I'm Baptist."

"Ha, and I'm Beyonce'," the mayor retorted. "I witnessed that little verbal exchange between you and William on the sidewalk this morning."

With a shrug of his shoulders, Cash replied, "last time I checked, this is a free country. If that is why you wanted to talk to me, I'll just be on my way."

"As much of a treat as it will be to see the back of you in a few minutes, I thought it only fair to bring you in and tell you this face to disgusting face. Yes, Mr. Waddell, this is indeed a free country, but this city is mine. While you are free to say anything that you choose, you are not free from the consequences of your words. I'd appreciate it if you'd show my nephew a little more respect when you see him out and about. Everyone, including human waste such as yourself, deserves to live in peace."

"Now wait just a minute," Cash began to protest, but couldn't finish as Ruth's voice got louder to drown him out.

"I know much more than you realize about the witless criminal enterprise that you and your worthless father are running out in the county. As Tennyson County has its own governing body, I look the other way, understanding that the matter is outside of my jurisdiction. However, and understand every word I say, I will have you searched and detained every single time you enter the city limits of Noeware, if I get the slightest inkling that one of my citizens is being harassed by such filth as you again. Do I make myself perfectly clear? Did you drive here today, Cash? Should I have Chief Thomas check the VIN number on your vehicle?"

"I walked."

"Slithered more like," the mayor continued. "You know, I had high hopes when you were born. Your mother was a very close friend of mine. She was a lovely woman, deserving of so much better than the hell you and your father put her through."

"Leave my mother out of this, Ruth."

"That's Mayor Blakely to you, Mr. Waddell," the mayor scanned him from head to toe, "perhaps I should have an officer frisk you while you're here."

"Wait a damn minute, I have rights."

"Currently Cash, you have the right to get the hell out of my office and I would take a little time to consider our conversation if I were you. This is not a threat. It's a word of warning: make trouble for my family, I am coming for yours."

Ruth reached into the top left drawer of her desk and pulled out a book with a fancy pink bow on it. She looked up at Cash Waddell with a mischievous smirk, as her assistant Tina returned to the office door, "I got you a little gift this morning, I thought it might come in handy." The mayor handed the thesaurus to Cash and said, "now, please get out of my office, you illiterate sphincter, and let me get on with the work of the people of Noeware. Actually, that phrase can be the first thing you look up in your new book."

As Cash squeezed past Tina Hansard to exit Ruth Blakely's

office, the assistant whispered, "She thinks you're an ignorant asshole."

"Yeah, I got that," Cash replied, agitated, as he left, so hot from anger he was practically steaming.

JUST BEFORE LUNCH, TINA HANSARD WALKED INTO THE mayor's office navigating her way with a white cane in her right hand and struggling to cradle a cardboard box with her left arm. She sat the box down on the edge of Ruth Blakely's desk.

"Here is that box of extension cords you were asking about. I have no idea which cord is going to be long enough to reach from your new lamp to the power outlet, but I will be happy to help figure it out after lunch."

"No need," replied the mayor as she stood and opened the box, "I'll go through them myself."

"Sounds good," Tina replied as she headed towards the door, "Allison Edwards is here for her 11:45 appointment."

"Yes, I've been looking forward to speaking with Ms. Edwards. Please, send her in. Enjoy your lunch."

Allison entered the office, enthralled by how expertly Tina Hansard maneuvered around the furniture. Every item that sat on the visually impaired assistant's desk appeared to be in a precise place so that it could be easily located. Allison was so impressed by the ability of blind people to flow through a world built more for sighted people.

"Good morning, Ms. Edwards," the mayor greeted her while standing beside the open box of cords. Ruth lightly held her walker with her left hand and grabbed a black cord with her right. "You'll excuse me if I sort through this mess while we chat, won't you?"

"Of course," Allison replied, while watching the cord slip from Ruth's hand and hit the worn carpet. Making a quick move, Allison went to pick the cord up.

Loudly, Ruth said, "Ms. Edwards, one should always ask if they can be of help, rather than assume that a person needs it. I may require the use of a walker, but my disability has never been a crutch."

"I'm so sorry", Allison responded a little embarrassed, "I didn't mean ..."

"Shhhhh, never mind. I trust that your meeting this morning with my brother-in-law was productive?" the mayor asked as she bent at the knees to carefully (and painfully) retrieve the power cord.

"It was, very much so," though Allison was still reeling from having read the story written about her in the paper and seeing no mention of Jess at all. How in the world did the hotel know about her? "He has actually invited me to join his family for dinner at their house this evening."

"Has he now? You're in luck, my sister Cora is an incredible cook. I hope you don't have cholesterol issues," Ruth teased with a sly smile. "Now, you aren't here to discuss my sister's culinary skills. I assume that you have some questions that you'd like to ask me about our lovely town. I'll be happy to have some sandwiches brought in for lunch, if you are hungry. It is almost that time."

"That is so kind, but I did just have a biscuit at the Journal," she said, so glad that food had been offered after not eating for the better part of 24 hours. "Is your family originally from Noeware, Mayor Blakely?"

"Oh yes," Ruth responded as she unwrapped another cord from the menagerie in her box.

"And it's you, your sister's family …"

"Yes, that about covers it. But enough about my family, Ms. Edwards, do you have a family of your own?"

Understanding the mayor's desire to change the subject, Allison complied, "Well, my mother lives in Alpharetta, she is more suited to suburban life than I am. My partner, Jessica, and I live not far from the Little Five Points area, in Atlanta's Old Fourth Ward."

"Yes," Ruth replied with a nod, "I am familiar with the place. Jessica didn't accompany you on your trip to South Georgia?"

"I'm afraid that she had to work, but you don't want me to bore you with my life story, either. Do you mind if I ask you some questions for my article? Like, where the city of Noeware got its rather unusual name?"

Ruth sighed, obviously disappointed by the generic nature of Allison's first question. "Well, let's see, you must first understand that our town's forefathers possessed more narcissism than they did foresight," Ruth began as Allison pulled out a small tape recorder. "The patriarchs of both the Noem family and the Ware family were critical in establishing this city as the county seat. It never occurred to those simpletons that their names combined, to establish the city's name, would forever open its citizens up to ridicule. I mean, we could have just as easily been the City of Warnoe, but then who would have ever heard of us?"

Allison understood the mayor's point, as people in Atlanta made countless jokes about the city's name whenever they were made aware of it, but they never forgot it.

"The Ware and Noem families were nut farmers, mostly peanuts and pecans. They possessed hundreds of slaves to work the countless acres of crops. This is why Tennyson County has such a large population of African Americans."

This came as no surprise to Allison, as anyone familiar with southern history knew that the old confederate states had once been partial to slave ownership. She prodded Ruth to continue, "And the Tennyson family? I am guessing that the county was named for them?"

"Well, Abe Tennyson, that is a whole other story. Are you familiar with the Billie Holiday song 'Strange Fruit'? The song depicts southern trees as having grown strange fruit, meaning people hung from the limbs. See that big oak tree out front? The one on the front lawn of this building?" Ruth and Allison gazed out the window. "I want you to look closely at that tree Ms. Edwards. You see, southern family trees, much like that ancient oak out front, don't have linear branches, they are crooked, almost woven through each other. Generations of people are born in this area, many never leave. Often, a family's history can be traced back to ancestors common to other families here. Abe Tennyson learned this lesson firsthand. He discovered that his wife Delila was having an affair with one of the slaves who worked on his plantation. Let's just say, the crops were not the only thing in Tennyson County that summer to go nuts. As the story goes, Abe couldn't live with the shame of his wife willingly sleeping with a negro, so he accused the slave of rape. Obviously, a colored man couldn't get away with raping a white woman, even if there was no proof that a crime was committed. So, Jacob, a man not even dignified in the history books with a surname, was brought to this actual building and hung from that very oak tree. The whole county came out to watch the spectacle. That summer, for almost two days, in the horrific South Georgia heat, Jacob was the strange fruit that dangled from that tree. Later, it became obvious that Delila Tennyson was pregnant. Assuming that there was a good chance that the child was fathered by Jacob, and not himself, Abe Tennyson threw his wife down a flight of stairs. The purpose of this violence was to abort the child, but Delila's neck was broken in the process. She died instantly."

Allison, still staring at the tree through the window, was completely crushed by this story. "What happened to Abe Tennyson? Was he tried for the murder of his wife?"

"He was given a choice. Leave his plantation to his extended family and flee Georgia or face a murder trial that was sure to embarrass all his relatives. As I am sure you can guess, his family didn't leave the choice up to him. He had left town for good before the next sunrise. As the story goes, he started a new plantation, funded by family money, over the state line in Alabama."

"My God," Allison exclaimed, still looking at the oak tree in disbelief. It's woven branches like a quilt on so many southern beds. "It is amazing that a place that held so much racial tension has come so far. I mean, look at you, the African American female mayor."

"Well now, that progress didn't come swiftly or easily. I grew up in the county, but the colored people went to school in the city limits. It was a long walk, but we made the trek daily. Walking quickly, day in and day out, passing that oak every morning and afternoon. They'd yell 'tar baby" as I went to grade school, 'darkie' before I went to Atlanta to finish high school, even called me 'jigaboo' when I came home from Georgia State University."

"But you were never afraid?" Allison asked.

"Of course, I was afraid. There will always be hate directed at 'the first' of anything, and I was a twofer."

A twofer, the mayor repeated to herself, a word reminding her of another time.

"But you ran for mayor." Allison said.

"And I won. For the first time in my life, I saw the fear in *their* faces," Ruth said as her mind wandered to the day of her election. "They were terrified, Ms. Edwards, and you want to know why? Because generations of black folks meandered through life in this county being treated like second class citizens, or worse. The day I took my oath of office, the story of Jacob and Delila was on my mind, as ghosts of the past linger in the south. I held my head up high, plastered a smile on my face, raised my right hand, looked up at that tree and knew that a new day had dawned." A crescendo formed in the voice of Ruth Blakely as she continued.

"After all those years of tar baby," she continued with a grimace — and got louder.

"Jigaboo," she said with a snarl, even louder.

"Darkie," she spat in a near yell.

Ruth's grip on the extension cord was so tight that her

knuckles had almost turned white.

"I had reached the highest elected office in this city, but to many, I still had the word 'nigga' tattooed on my forehead. They simply weren't prepared for anyone different acquiring any power, let alone becoming mayor. I suppose they never considered that there would be a day that THIS darkie would be the one holding the noose, and I've spent a lifetime taking names."

The look on the mayor's face was of a woman consumed by the ghosts of a dark past. A woman who had overcome obstacles, and who had an intimate relationship with hurt. A woman who was sure of herself, and wore every slur thrown at her as a reason to push herself further — a reason for vengeance. "'Ruthless' is what they call me now. Have you heard that one? Well, Ms. Edwards, sometimes you must give the people what they expect. Far be it for me to let them down."

Allison sat down on a bench outside of City Hall, having just left Mayor Ruth Blakely's office. She didn't quite know how to feel about her meeting with the woman. However, she did now understand how the mayor acquired her nickname. Allison wasn't accustomed to hearing the words used by the mayor, Atlanta just wasn't a place where one would feel free to say such things. She exhaled, realizing that she had been holding onto a breath since leaving the third-floor office, and listened to the whistle blow from the ever-present old steam engine passing by.

Wooooooot

CHAPTER 6
TENNYSON COUNTY, TENNYSON ESTATE

The early evening sun was still blazing over the two-story white slat board house that was home to Harrison (Harry) Tennyson. Not for the first time, he wondered why on earth he and his wife kept a house so large for just two people. Ah yes, because Camille insisted on it. To her, Tennyson Place and its history meant status. It was part of his family's plantation dating back to the founding of Tennyson County, and she had seamlessly added that trophy to her mantlepiece. She had no issue with notions that preserving overt reminders of plantation history was repugnant. She found those ideas merely faddish. Harry was less certain; he had always felt a bit of unease with the idea of his family's history of what could only be called human trafficking. That unease was insufficient to offset the much greater discomfort of countering the opinions of his wife. While their children were young, he found plenty of justification for remaining in the five-bedroom manor house. That rationale grew increasingly tenuous the longer the kids had been out of the house (and so far, none had contributed any grandchildren to pick up the slack). Still, it was easier to keep the place than to risk an ordeal with Camille. He did whatever he could to avoid dealing with Camille when she was upset, and she was often upset.

The land adjacent to the house was covered in peanut crops for as far as the eye could see. Hundreds and hundreds of acres of peanut plants tended to by a large crew of workers. In the old days, workers lived on the land they farmed, these days they came in during long, often grueling work shifts. It took an endless supply of laborers to run a farm such as this, as the pay was poor, and the working conditions were worse. The Georgia heat was unforgiving, the chores were backbreaking, and Tennyson County wasn't exactly the entertainment capital of the state. No one wanted to keep a job like this for long.

Harry Tennyson was born and raised in this house — literally born in it. Hospital deliveries had been by far the norm by the time he came around in the late 1950s, but he had arrived faster than expected, and the nearest hospital in those days was a good 30 minutes away. Ironically, this was the only time he'd be early for any occasion. Harrison was known for his tardiness, but not many teased him about it. He was a much too serious man to accept even lighthearted banter.

His family, direct descendants of one of the county's founding fathers, remained very prominent not just in South Georgia, but all around the Southeastern United States. Harry was the most senior member of the county commission. His younger sister, Claire, had the aptitude and diligence to do just about anything she wanted. But she never could break orbit and leave Harry behind. She had contented herself with pouring her copious ambition into the role of general manager of the Grand Hotel. They were not just siblings; they were one another's closest friend and confidante. That's what happens in a household like the one the Tennyson kids had grown up in; even at a young age they were acutely aware that Tennyson business stayed inside the walls of Tennyson Place. They had only one another to rely on when dealing with an uncertain future. Their parents certainly weren't there for them. They only took notice of the kids to briefly acknowledge and tally their not-infrequent public successes. For Harry, these included Varsity wins (though he always – privately – preferred more passive, some would say intellectual pursuits). Had Claire's physical power matched that of her wit, she'd have been much better suited to the gridiron than her brother. As it was, she had to content herself with domination in debate club and giving a barnburner of a valedictorian address that would have gone viral if smartphones had been around at the time. Not a few of those present expected a future in politics for Claire, but once Harry tied himself to Camille, and thus to Tennyson County, Claire never quite found her way clear to move on.

Harry married Camille Archer in his mid-20s. Camille was as smart and cunning as she was gorgeous. She was well known and connected in her own right, coming from the family of one of the largest tobacco farmers in the region. Being raised as an only child, Camille was used to getting what she wanted, and what she wanted was Harry Tennyson. This union created a clash between Camille and Claire which remains today. Even though she married a worthy man herself,

Claire lived for her brother, her husband wisely chose to take a backseat. Claire and her husband Stan never had children of their own, but Claire played a large role in the lives of her two nieces, Gail and Meg, as if she were their third parent.

Gail took on the role of front desk manager at the Grand Hotel, a position she more than earned, not one given to her out of nepotism. Meg attended medical school at Emory University in Atlanta and became a Hospitalist at Noeware General Hospital. Both young women understood that Tennyson County was home and that they were expected to live up to the family's reputation of hard work and philanthropy.

Tonight, Harry Tennyson was home alone, beads of sweat forming along the hairline of his full silver mane. The old air conditioning unit, installed in the house over 20 years ago, was struggling to stay ahead of the early autumn heat. While he puffed on a cigar and drank the last few drops of the watered-down lemonade in his glass, he heard the familiar sound of a car heading up the driveway.

The front doorbell chimed, and Harry headed in that direction to greet his guest. Long gone were the days of maids and housekeepers running around the house. Harry saw no reason to keep up such pretenses, when he basically lived alone, Camille being constantly on the road. He peeked through the peephole to see his sister, Claire Montgomery, had arrived, as she often did when she finished work for the day at the Grand Hotel. "Well, you're a little earlier than usual, Claire."

"I have had the day of days, Harry. What are we drinking?" Claire asked as the two of them headed to the study.

"Scotch for me, you good with that?"

"Make mine a double, please. That Daisy Wei at the front desk just may be the death of me. My God, it's hot in here. Are you conserving energy or is the air conditioner on the blink?"

"You're like a broken record, you've been saying the same thing every night since Daisy started two years ago. Why are you dealing with her anyway, isn't that what you pay Gail for?" Harry asked as he poured and handed Claire her drink. "Also, I'll have you know, there is nothing wrong with the temperature in here. It is just that hot outside."

"Your daughter, Gail, covers up and makes excuses for absolutely every mishap that Daisy has, Harry. Anyway, enough about Daisy. The girl from Atlanta arrived last night."

"She did, and you didn't think to let me know?"

"We are incredibly short staffed, Harry. Excuse me if alerting you to a guest's arrival is not my top priority."

"This is not just any guest, Claire. I would have thought you'd have made this a priority."

"Look, big brother, we are running around that hotel like mad, doing our very best to accommodate the reporters who are camping out because of you. I'd appreciate it if you would show a little appreciation."

"I'm sorry. You're right. I really do appreciate everything that you, Gail, and even Daisy are doing. I know it can't be easy to field questions all day about me." Harrison pulled his cellphone out of his pocket and checked the screen.

"It's not easy, but it'll be worth it in the end. Have you thought about how you plan to make contact with the girl? I'm sorry, do you need to take that call?"

"No. It's Steve McDonald. He's been blasting my phone for days. I've told the congressman a thousand times to communicate through Camille. I'm too busy to deal with all of this. Now, where were we? Oh yes, the girl from Atlanta. Honestly, I thought I would let Gail and Meg figure that out. Afterall, all of this was their idea."

"Congressman McDonald? I thought that mess was over with. Is he still begging forgiveness for his little indiscretion with Camille? It's been several years now, for Christ's sake."

"I would assume that's the case. I can't stand a man who grovels. I thought that our discussion of the matter had put an end to it. I guess in his mind, it didn't."

"Well, I will deal with the congressman so you may take that item off your list. Now, back to the other matter, I think you're putting an awful lot of faith in your daughters, Harry. I hope they broach the subject carefully. The last thing we need is to be shot down and mentioned unfavorably in the article she is here to write."

"Faith in my daughters is exactly what I have, Claire. They'll do just fine. Want another scotch?" Harry asked as he shook his empty glass.

"I better not. Lord knows I need not smell of liquor in case I get called back to the hotel. Besides, if I don't make an appearance at home, Stan is going to think I moved. Too many late nights at the hotel and all that."

"Understood. I'll walk you to the door; be careful driving home."

As Claire's car drove out of sight at the bottom of the hill, Harry poured himself one more scotch. At least, just one more is what he told himself. Then again, every night he told himself 'just one more' about half a dozen times. He drank to fortune, misfortune, and everything in between. He was well aware that he was a functioning alcoholic, but 'functioning' was the key word. He was in complete control of his words and actions and did not consider his drinking a problem as long as he was. Well, completely in control except for those nights. The nights that sleep never arrived. The nights that he and Claire's older sister took up occupancy in his head. The nights he wondered 'what if.' What if Olivia hadn't been taken so soon? What if the eldest had lived? Who would they each be now? What paths would they be on? Would Olivia be the reining matriarch of the Tennyson family, or would she have moved on without much interest in family ties at all? The situation was far too tragic to dwell on, but for the better part of five decades, dwell on it is what Harry did. The happenings of one afternoon, over 50 years ago, completely changed the trajectory of a dynasty. Harry knew it. Claire knew it. The entire county knew it. Olivia, not Harry, was the golden child — the great hope — and like an extinguished candle, she was gone in a puff of smoke, and the wisps of that smoke would shape a community forever.

CHAPTER 7
TENNYSON COUNTY, 1972

The dry leaves crunched under the weight of giggling teenage girls on that cooler than normal autumn day in the woods of Tennyson County, Ga. The remanence of dead foliage that had slowly rained down to the dirt floor, now carpeted the path that the girls took to the bank of Owen's Creek. The girls had been there a thousand times together. It was their place. Three pieces of an unlikely puzzle, two ivory and one ebony, they just fit together perfectly. Having just finished school for the day, one of the girls was swinging a trash filled brown bag that had served as a makeshift lunch pail, a bag that would be reused until it fell apart, another carried a *Partridge Family* lunchbox, her celebrity crush David Cassidy featured prominently on the side.

While two of the girls practically skipped down the leaf littered path, they were careful not to leave the third too far behind. She, the ebony girl, struggled to keep up, as she had an increasingly dramatic limp, an unfortunate result of untreated hip dysplasia that had plagued her since birth. A condition that her family's abject poverty, and her mother's general lack of concern, had resulted in severe arthritis. The inflammation got worse by the year, it seemed, though the girl never said a word about it, nor used it as an excuse not to go toe to toe with her peers in any activity. The other two girls admired their third musketeer greatly for this, though they seldom mentioned it, as it simply wasn't a matter any of them felt was significant enough to warrant discussion. Ruth had a limp — so what?

As the girls approached the ice-cold water of the creek, ice cold by South Georgia standards anyway, the teasing began. "Mary, does your daddy know you are here this afternoon, or did you tell him you were at the library again?" "Mary's daddy is going to be THRILLED to learn that she spent the afternoon with a black chick." The girls cackled, all three of them, though Mary knew that their teases had a ring of truth to them. Her daddy was the kind of man that thought Archie Bunker from *All in the Family* was a character to idolize, not mock and laugh at. He blamed all his life's troubles on the black or Hispanic men that he was convinced were trying to take over HIS country. Mary shared none of these thoughts. Ruth and Olivia were her chosen sisters, as far as she was concerned, and nothing could break their bond. Three young girls, equal in every way, friends until the end.

Suddenly a bit anxious, Mary took the good-natured teasing a little too seriously, "Maybe I should get home. I really do have a lot of homework to get finished if I am going to be able to enjoy Founders' Day weekend."

"We were just messing with you, Mary, you can hang out a little longer," Ruth said, feeling a little guilty for upsetting her friend.

"Your daddy won't even be looking for you for an hour or so, right? He never expects you home directly after the school bell rings," Olivia said by way of encouraging her friend to enjoy a few more minutes outside of her unhappy home life.

"Nah, I better get a move on, but I will see you both this weekend, right?"

"If our lunch with that queen of England happens to get cancelled, I reckon we might just make it," Ruth said, causing all three girls to giggle gleefully. "Maybe we'll just make excuses, 'Liz, this here Ruth Blakely from Georgia. No, not that Georgia over in the Soviet Union, the other one, in America, you know that country that kicked your tea sipping butt. We sure would love to come eat some crumpets with you, but Founder's Day is this weekend. I am afraid that we must send our regrets.'"

The three girls continued to laugh, as they shared hugs and bid Mary farewell for the day. The very last thing that Mary wanted to do was anything to cause her daddy not to let her attend the Founder's Day festivities. This weekend was always THE weekend in Tennyson County. She just had to be there. Regretfully, she paved a path back up through the woods, and back to a reality that caused her soul to weep. Ruth and Olivia were her family, her daddy was a disabled racist, bent on keeping her locked up in the house, friendless, hopeless, desperate for a way out.

Now, sitting side by side on the bank of Owen's Creek, Ruth and Olivia stared at the ripples in the water created by the tiny pebbles Olivia tossed one after the other. Almost hypnotized by the natural kaleidoscope, Ruth spoke first, keeping her eyes firmly on the water, careful not to make eye contact, "You know you don't have to pay me any mind this weekend, your daddy and them wouldn't be any happier with you walking with a colored girl any more than Mary's ole man would."

"Ruth Blakely, don't you ever say such things to me! And stop that country talk; you are better than that. You are the smartest girl in school, though many would never admit it and the bar isn't very high. The sky is the limit for what you can accomplish. I am proud to stand next to you anywhere. I love you, silly."

The speech took Ruth a little by surprise but wasn't exactly shocking. She knew Olivia loved her. All three girls had love for each other. However, this felt different, heavier, more emotionally charged, heartfelt and soulful. This feeling was only amplified by Olivia, also keeping her vision focused on the creek, taking Ruth's hand. The girls sat this way silently for what seemed to both of them like an eternity and a split second.

"Can I braid your hair?" Ruth asked.

"You always want to braid my hair, Ruth Blakely. I tell you what, sit right there, and I will braid your hair."

"Yeah?"

"Sure. You just sit there and pretend you are at one of those fine beauty parlors in Atlanta," Olivia said as she began running her fingers through Ruth's hair.

The two sat in silence for several minutes, listening to the creek, the birds, the distant train whistle. It was the perfect fall afternoon. The sun was bright. There wasn't a significant chance of rain, only soft white clouds interrupted the flawless blue sky. "You know what I think about when I see a cloud on a pretty day," Olivia asked. "I think that you could ride that cloud straight to heaven."

"Well, I don't think that's how it works," Ruth replied.

"Well, just suppose that it did."

"Well, if we're just supposing ..."

In a moment of bravery, Ruth released her focus on the sky, turned to face her best friend, and kissed the girl on the cheek. Though she prepared herself to be rebuffed, Olivia responded in kind by providing Ruth with the first kiss on the mouth that she had ever received from another human being. The intensity of the moment was thick, and it hung in the air like Georgia humidity. In this moment, nothing else existed but the two of them. Two girls, becoming young women, experiencing a pure love that neither of them had ever known before.

Though it felt like it, they weren't the only two people in the world. In fact, they weren't the only two people in the woods at that moment. Crackling leaves sounded an alarm, as the boys emerged from behind the shrubbery, bushes left lackluster by the approaching winter. Suddenly, the girls were surrounded by three boys, a gang of misfits obviously being led by Jeremiah Waddell, who separated their faces with his head, and spoke with vile breath, "Look what we have here boys, a twofer, she's a dyke and a darkie lover."

An all-encompassing fear filled the bodies of both Ruth and Olivia as two of the boys put their hands on them, bringing them to their feet, in a more painful manner for

Ruth than Olivia. Attempting to pull away from the group, Ruth hurled her inflamed legs away from the side of the creek, toward the path that had brought them to this place initially. "Olivia, run. I'll be okay," she said luring two of the boys away from her friend.

With tears forming in her eyes, more out of fear for her friend, who she knew could suffer a much harsher punishment for their indiscretion than herself, Olivia ran in the opposite direction, down the length of the creek, past the area that was familiar. Unable to hear the dead leaves over the sound of her own heart pounding, she urged her feet to move faster than she thought they were capable of running. Pursuing her, and not from a great distance, was Jeremiah, who was taunting and teasing her with every step. "Somebody just needs a good man. I'll screw the dyke out of you, darkie lover. Twofer." He seemed to have assumed the role of a hunting dog who had a raccoon firmly in sight.

Normally, Olivia wouldn't have been the least bit afraid of Jeremiah Waddell, but today was different. She was afraid that he'd tell everyone what he saw. She was afraid that he'd hurt her. She was afraid of the crazed look in his eyes. She was afraid, period.

Approaching a thicket of trees, Olivia saw the opportunity to find a hiding place. The situation was less than ideal, as she could hear Jeremiah's foot plants close behind. She didn't think there was any way that she could hide well enough to remain safe for long, if she could hide at all with him so close. Woooooooot, came the sound of The G.R.I.T. from a distance. The wail from the steam engine seemed to distract the boy just enough for Olivia to jump into a nearby ditch and hide under a bunch of hanging roots. Trying her best to silence her heavy and panicked breathing, Olivia waited, listened, and prayed.

Stunned, Olivia was convinced that she had just released her bladder, but that made no sense at all. The moisture was cold, seeping in from the outside of her long corduroy skirt, rather than being warm like freshly eliminated urine making its way out from beneath her clothes. But how could this be? Owen's Creek was the only body of water in these woods, at least as far as Olivia knew, so where was this water coming from? Then she heard it, the unmistakable sound of a truck driving down the road, a road that couldn't be more than a few yards from where she was hiding. Had she run that far? Was it possible that she had made her way through the woods to the scenic highway in the county?

Olivia decided to chance it. She stood up and ran with a strength she didn't know that she had, straight down the length of the unpaved drainage ditch, toward sunlight that shone like a beacon through the trees. She could still hear Jeremiah behind her, but his pace had begun to slow as he realized that Olivia would soon be out in the open, and whatever he had planned for her would be virtually impossible if they were to be seen by someone. Still, she did not let up on her own speed. She ran full on until she had made it to the road. The ditch had been dug years ago to allow for drainage off the country road. Olivia just hadn't recognized it, having never seen it from inside the woods. She now knew exactly where she was, coming up behind Frog Rock, a large granite boulder shaped like an amphibian, but four times the size of a human, and there was help. Oh, dear merciful God, there was help!

She ran directly to the light blue Chevy Nova, knowing exactly who it belonged to, as she recognized nearly everyone's vehicle in a town this small, and she risked a scream, that came out more as a muffled whimper.

The whimper was enough to catch the man's attention. "Olivia Tennyson, is that you, girl? What in the world are you doing out here all by yourself, and why do you look like you've been running from the devil?"

Olivia, winded from the run, had trouble answering the man's questions. He noticed the condition she was in and directed her to have a seat on the passenger's side of the Nova's bench seat. "I've been out working in the county. I have a cooler of water in the trunk. I was just stopping to dump it in the ditch. You want a cup?"

Olivia nodded with appreciation as she slowly caught her breath. The man went to the trunk of his car, after patting her on the shoulder to reassure her that everything was going to be alright. Sitting sideways on the car seat with the door open and her legs facing the woods, Olivia realized that Jeremiah Waddell must have gone back to meet his friends, as he was nowhere in sight. She was all alone on this country road, with this man that she knew, but not well. She worried about what had become of Ruth, just as she began to wonder what was taking the man so long to pour a cup of water.

Olivia made a move to stand up, deciding that walking back to town, while the sun was still up, was probably her best move. If she stayed on the public road, out in the open, she would likely be okay. But, before she could stand, she got a whiff of an unfamiliar scent. It was chemical, but not a chemical she knew. She looked around for the source of the smell but was unable to turn her head. In disbelief, Olivia realized that the smell was coming from a rag, a rag placed over her nose and mouth, while the man's other hand was holding her head and neck in place. This can't really be happening, she thought to herself, as her struggle, that was half-hearted at best due to her run through the woods, became futile. She made a last attempt to wave for help towards the woods, hoping that perhaps Jeremiah was spying on her from a distance, but no such luck. The last thing she saw, before she fell into a deep sleep, was the hand of Craig Burton, that weird crop pest exterminator that had arrived in Tennyson County offering his services last year.

Craig lay Olivia's listless body into the open trunk of his car, turning a rake over so that it wouldn't puncture her porcelain skin. He closed the trunk, looked around carefully to be sure that he had not been seen by anyone, sat behind the steering wheel and directed the car down the deserted road away from Noeware and out of the county. So far, he had gotten away with an abduction like this once before, a little over a year ago, and he intended to get away with this one. He knew the risk was great, as Olivia belonged to one of the most prominent families in the area, but the potential payoff made it worth it. So far, no one seemed to suspect the real reason that he had ventured to South Georgia in the first place. Lucrative, he thought to himself, that's what Tennyson County was, and one of its namesakes was unconscious in his trunk right now.

CHAPTER 8
TENNYSON COUNTY, WASHINGTON RESIDENCE, PRESENT DAY

The sun was slowly setting, laying a pink hue over the well-worn wooden house. The outside was painted a hunter green, with a burgundy trim, a color scheme that was a throwback to the early 1990s but added a nice charm in this setting. Though the house was two stories, it would barely be noticed in the land of McMansions known as Atlanta. In miniature, the place would make the perfect home for a family of dolls, but as it was, it was home to Carl Washington, the Editor of the *Noeware Journal*, his wife Cora and their young grandchildren. Tonight, two more places would be set at the dinner table, as Allison Edwards and Billy Washington thumped along the hole pitted gravel driveway in Billy's barely functioning Pontiac Sunbird (circa early 1980s).

"Thank you for being patient with me, G.H. The battery cables stay loose on this heap. Sometimes, I have to get out and raise the hood at stop lights."

"No apologies necessary. I am just happy that we didn't have to call a taxi to bring us out here for dinner."

"A taxi? In Noeware, GA? Girl, honey ... ummm ... G.H., we got one car with one driver to take the stranded around town, and it ain't a yellow cab. Ole Hank and his pickup truck are as close as you are gonna get to hailing any vehicle on the side of one of our roads."

Allison giggled, unable to tell if this was another of Billy's teases, or if "Ole Hank" really was the preferred mode of transportation of the car challenged in Tennyson County. "Perhaps I better get Hank's number from you later, just in case I find myself in need of a ride."

Billy stopped the car behind a navy-blue Honda Civic parked in the uncovered driveway. He jumped out first, obviously eager to get inside to see his family. Allison followed close behind, locking the door on her side of the car as she exited.

"You are not in Atlanta anymore, G.H., there ain't nobody gonna go through this car while we are inside," Billy said looking over the top of the car at Allison while shaking his head.

"Habit, sorry."

As they walked up the steps to the front porch, the door flew open, startling Allison, but putting a huge grin on Billy's face, "Hey, Mama!"

"Well, y'all better get yourselves in here, it's hotter than blue blazes out there," Cora Washington said as she gave her son a hug that he had to bend a good foot and a half to receive. "I ain't never seen such a pitiful excuse for a vehicle in all my days, Billy. I'll worry myself to an early grave thinkin' you are gonna be stranded on the side of the road somewhere. Did they have a clearance sale at the landfill?"

"I'm having trouble deciding whether or not you like my new car, mama," replied Billy sarcastically, "I can't afford much on tips at the diner."

"New car? My heavenly days, child. That car ain't been new since Abraham Lincoln was in office." Cora glanced beside her son and continued, "How rude of me, you must be Allison. I'm Cora Washington and I am so happy to finally meet you. Welcome to my home."

Making his way slowly from the living room, and his recliner where he was watching CNN, Carl Washington stepped into the kitchen, still trying to stand upright after getting out of the chair. "Well Cora, you going to let our guests get out of the doorway and offer them something to drink, or are we serving supper on the threshold?"

Rolling her eyes at her husband, but grinning at the same time, Cora looked in the direction of the kitchen table. "Why don't you two go ahead and have a seat. I am just finishin' up supper. I hope y'all are hungry, I may have gotten carried away." Cora walked over to the stove, where a few steaming pots, producing an incredible aroma, promised a delicious homecooked dinner.

Allison was struck by the difference between Ms. Cora and her sister, Ruth. Where Ruth had been hard, almost cold in nature, Cora was like a ray of sunshine. She had a kind presence about her that just made you feel comforted. Ruth was very no nonsense. Cora was plain spoken, while her sister had the tone of the higher educated, proper. Allison wondered how two people, raised in the same family, could be so entirely opposite.

Carl Washington took a seat at the head of his table, a place that was obviously reserved for him, "Allison, are you learning much about our illustrious town so far?"

"Honestly, Mr. Washington, with every conversation that I have, I am left with more questions than answers."

With a chuckle, Carl Washington responded, "First off, no more of this Mr. Washington business, my name is Carl. Mr. Washington was my daddy; may he rest in peace. Now, questions, you say, anything I can clear up right fast for you?"

"Well, this may seem strange, but I am very curious about a woman I met when getting off the bus entering town yesterday."

"Is that so? Noeware doesn't have a lot of anything, let alone a welcoming committee, pray tell who was this woman?"

"I think she said her name was Miss Willa, and everyone in town seemed to know her."

"Well, she's crazier than a loon, everybody knows it. Nuttier than a fruitcake," Billy chimed in. "They say she was never the same after Marlena got possessed by the devil, the first time, on *Days of Our Lives*."

WITH THE CRASH OF A PAN ON HER STOVE, CORA LOUDLY interrupted, "Billy, help me bring these bowls over. I ain't spent the better part of a day fixin' this food for it to get cold before the first bite. And you know we don't call folks crazy in this house. If we had every nut in Tennyson County committed, we'd need the world's biggest insane asylum, and the state closed that nearly two decades ago. Besides, you're the one with the *Days of Our Lives* addiction. You ain't stopped moanin' since it went to streaming on the computer."

"Well, it just ain't natural," Billy responded. "A man's gotta see his stories, and the stories belong on the TV."

"Lawd, don't anybody tell this fool that *Peyton Place* started out as a book," his mama teased.

"Soap operas, in a book? Blasphemy!" Billy retorted.

Carl Washington looked at his wife with a loving smile as he said, "Well Cora, what do we have here?"

What "we had here", was a virtual feast: cube steak and brown gravy, rice, homemade biscuits, stewed squash and onions, collard greens, and sliced tomatoes. Cora made herself busy by pouring drinks for everyone, sweet tea of course. She yelled for her grandchildren, Alex and Alisha, who soon joined the group after washing their hands and jumping all over their Uncle Billy with excitement. The children looked to Allison to be about twelve years old. "Well, are you going to say grace Carl, or are you going to watch the last of the steam rise out of that rice?" Cora asked Carl with the proud look a person gets when preparing a near perfect meal for the family.

"Ms. Cora, you have outdone yourself," Allison said, as her mouth all but watered.

"Well, I reckon Mama Jo did teach me one or two things," Cora replied with a smile.

"Oh, was your mother a good cook, too?"

"Oh yes. In her day, mama could turn an empty pantry into a gourmet meal."

"I am sure a meal like this brings back lots of good memories. I am sure you miss her."

"Miss her? Lawd, she won't give me time to miss her. I am over at that house at least twice a day checking on that old woman."

"Oh," Allison responded with surprise, "it's just that Ruth led me to believe that she was no longer with us."

Cora chuckled a little, "Well, the devil ain't called her home yet, child. Ruth doesn't like to talk much about mama and don't even get her started on Uncle J.B. He runs a pork processing business out on the outskirts of the county. You can't miss it at night, the security lights shine on that place like Fort Knox."

Billy nearly choked on his sweet tea, "Pork processing business? Why, that place ain't nothin' but a hog farm, and Mama Jo lives about a 10-minute drive from here, in the Honey Hole."

"Billy Washington, just because *they* call it the Honey Hole, don't mean we have to. It's been a long time since we were relegated to a colored part of town," Cora corrected.

Allison was becoming convinced that she could learn more about the history of Tennyson County by sitting around this dinner table than making frequent visits to City Hall.

AFTER DINNER (AND A LARGE HELPING OF HOMEMADE peach cobbler with vanilla ice cream so beautiful Allison had to ask to send a photo of it to Jess), Carl and Allison adjourned to the front porch while Billy helped his mother transfer food to Tupperware containers and wash the dishes. Allison had practically begged to help, but she was shooed from the kitchen with a determination she knew better than to try to resist. The children went upstairs to play video games before bed.

"Should I turn on the light," Allison asked once outside.

"Only if you want to attract pterodactyl-sized mosquitos," Carl Washington laughed.

"This has been a lovely evening, Carl. That meal was on another level."

"My Cora is the best cook in South Georgia, if you want my unbiased opinion."

"You'll get no argument from me on that point. Where did you two meet — in school?"

"Something like that. Believe it or not, as a kid I chased after her older sister, Ruth. There is just something about an older woman that drives a boy going through puberty wild."

With a laugh, Allison replied, "Ruth wasn't interested in a younger man, huh?"

"In all of my life, there was only one person in this whole world that Ruth Blakely had eyes for." The porch was nearly pitch dark, but Allison's eyes had adjusted enough to it to see that Carl Washington was gazing into another time. It was as if he was making a heavy withdrawal from his memory bank, "But that, my new friend, is not my tale to tell."

"Well, Billy is a whole lot of fun. I can see that he gets his quick wit from his mother," Allison said, in an attempt to change the subject.

"Billy is certainly one of a kind, that is for sure."

"If you don't mind me asking, and I mean no disrespect by this question at all, so feel free not to answer."

"Allison, are you going to ask or keep pre-apologizing for the rest of the night?"

"Well, I was just curious as to how you and Ms. Cora handled Billy's coming out?"

"Ah, well that is a mighty personal question, but seeing how well you fit in with the family, I am happy to answer it," he said with a wink. "In order for one to come OUT, one would have had to have ever been IN the closet. Billy was trying to prance around in Cora's high heels when he was a toddler. One day, over a coffee and cereal breakfast, Cora and I had a talk about it. She asked me two simple questions. First, did I believe that Billy was born gay. Well, he wasn't anywhere near puberty, so there wasn't anything sexual happening in his head yet. We knew that no one was messing with him in any inappropriate way, so there were no environmental issues that we could point to as a cause. So, he was obviously born to be who he was. You see, back in those days, folks still thought that molestation could lead to homosexuality. We've learned a lot since then. Her second question threw me for a loop but was the question that anyone raising a gay child should be asked. Did I believe that our God could make a mistake? Well, I am a Christian man Allison, and I am not arrogant enough to believe that I know better than my heavenly Father. With that, there was no need for us to discuss the issue further. Our job was to love our children unconditionally. Now, our older son Carlton Jr., he would have a lot more trouble coming to terms with Billy."

Just then, the screen door swung open, and Cora and Billy walked outside. "I can't stay out here; my hair will be flatter than a fritter for work tomorrow," Cora said.

"Kinky as a street whore more like," Carl mumbled under his breath while muffling a laugh.

"What did you say to me, Carl Washington?"

"Nothing, my love."

"Mmm hmm. Now, I hate to cut this evening short, but I have to open the hospital gift shop early in the morning."

"I have to get G.H. back to the hotel anyway. I am sure she has a lot of scoop to get out of the fine folks of Tennyson County tomorrow," Billy added.

After hugs all around, Carl and Cora walked inside, turning on the porch light so that Billy and Allison could see their way to the car. Over her shoulder Cora yelled, "Allison, I hope we'll see you in church Sunday. I hear Ruth has a fancy new hat."

In the car, Allison thanked Billy for driving her out for dinner, as they made their way back towards the road to Noeware.

MEANWHILE, UPSTAIRS THE WASHINGTON CHILDREN were going about their nightly rituals. Alisha was finishing up a paper for school that wasn't due until the following Monday. Unlike her brother, she wasn't the kind of kid who thrived on putting homework assignments off until the last possible moment. She did not work well under pressure but slept well knowing that her to-do list was complete. Alex, on the other hand, would wait until late the night before a due date to even start working on a task. Tonight, he procrastinated by playing his favorite video game, ***Social Annihilation***.

Alex had become a serious challenge to RedDragn111, the best player he had ever encountered while playing the game. While he had no idea who RedDragn111 was in real life, he was Alex's only real threat in the game and was quickly becoming a friend and confidante. Chatting while gaming was a perfect scenario for a socially awkward introvert like Alex. He had a friend that he could count on being there to listen, someone who shared many of his interests, someone who he didn't have to meet up with in the 3-dimentional world. The two were inseparable online, and that was more than enough for KidoutaNoeware2011 (Alex's gaming name).

While some gamers preferred the earbud and microphone approach to chatting, RedDragn111 and KidoutaNoeware2011 used a text method. This situation was much more appealing to Alex, as he would rather die than talk on the phone, and using a microphone to chat was the next worst thing. The written texts also allowed the two friends to speak privately, keeping their conversations away from the prying ears of parents, or grandparents, in Alex's case, not to mention twin sisters.

TENNYSON COUNTY, WASHINGTON RESIDENCE, PRESENT ...

RedDragn111: Nice shot there bro. you have time for one more game?

KidoutaNoewware2011: Nah, I gotta turn in soon the units will be up to make sure im asleep

RedDragn111: Bet. We can pick up tomorrow night. Thought anymore about that offer I made u?

KidoutaNoeware2011: Yeah what worries me is I'm not exactly popular

KidoutaNoeware2011: I don't know many kids that would b interested. I'm not even allowed to have TikTok cuz the units are afraid someone'll grab me or some shit

KidoutaNoeware2011: A couple of girls disappeared when they were kids so I gotta pay the price for that

RedDragn111: You don't THINK you know any kids that would be interested?

RedDragn111: Dude, you let them know you got the gear, your popularity will soar like a fuckin eagle.

RedDragn111: Trust me on this, you are gonna be THE MAN at school

KidoutaNoeware2011: Yeah?

RedDragn111: Hell yeah, dude! No cap!

KidoutaNoeware2011: Bet! Let's do it!

RedDragn111:YES, my dude!

CHAPTER 9
NOEWARE, GA, TENNYSON GENERAL HOSPITAL

A combination of cold air and anxiety hit Allison Edwards all at once upon entering the emergency department of Tennyson General Hospital. It felt as if the thermostat must be set on 58 degrees when she walked through the automatic exterior doors. Confusion set in, as she looked for the Check-in desk. Less than twenty minutes ago, Allison had been sound asleep, dreaming that she was a character in a Fannie Flagg novel, no doubt a reflection of the evening she had spent with the Washington family, when her cell's ringtone brought her to consciousness.

Her new friend Billy Washington had been attacked, the caller had informed her, and he was asking for her specifically. It took Allison a few minutes to register the voice of the caller as well as the information being conveyed. Was this part of her dream? Was it morphing into a nightmare? Unfortunately, she was wide awake, and an unfamiliar woman's voice was relaying a true scenario, which left Allison in a state of shock and terror.

Now, locating the person in charge of emergency check-in, Allison was pointed toward a door and given directions to the proper room. The halls of any hospital were a challenge, but this place was like a rat maze in a laboratory. She navigated two lefts and a right and assumed she had reached her destination when she arrived at an open door with a small crowd gathered around it. How in the world had this happened, Allison asked herself? Billy had just dropped her off a few hours ago at the Grand Hotel, and she assumed that he was headed back to his apartment for the evening.

"Allison, oh good you're here," Cora Washington said by way of greeting her, an exhausted look of worry and sadness in her eyes. "The doctors are in with him now. Let's you and me get a quick cup of coffee." Allison nodded and put her arm around the uniform clad mother of her friend, who was obviously already dressed for her shift at the hospital gift shop. "I'll fill you in on what I know on the way." Cora's husband Carl had obviously stayed behind at home with the children.

AS ALLISON AND CORA MADE THEIR WAY DOWN THE hallway, inside the hospital room, Dr. Meg Givens, her husband Dr. Don Givens, and Chief of Police Ernie Thomas were all huddled around the bed where Billy was holding court.

"You've got a few nasty bruises and two fractured ribs, but it looks like you escaped the most serious of possibilities," Meg Givens said as she made some notes on an electronic chart.

"You're really lucky that Willa Banks came along when she did. It looks like the attacker was worried about being identified," added Chief Thomas. "She may not be the most intimidating sort, but she obviously scared him off."

"Dr. Givens, phone call for you." Both Meg and Don looked up simultaneously, trying to determine which of them was being addressed. "I'm sorry, Dr. Meg Givens," nurse Rhonda Conner continued from her position at the doorway of the room.

"Thank you," Meg replied, as she headed out the door with Chief Thomas on her heels.

"I appreciate the statement Billy, get some rest. Oh, and you might want to stay out of that alley behind the club. You and I both know that there is nothing but trouble going on back there. I wouldn't want anyone to get the wrong idea that you were back there with the other folks cruising for …," Chief Thomas didn't finish his thought as he left the room. He figured his point had been made. "Oh yeah," he added over his shoulder, "remind Ms. Edwards that I still need that statement from her about someone following her," he chuckled under his breath.

Now, alone in the room together, Dr. Don Givens looked down at Billy Washington and asked flatly, "You didn't tell anyone that I had been back there as well before the attack, did you?"

"Lawd no, Dr. Feelgood, your little secret is safe with me,"

Billy replied with a nervous wink. "Besides, I didn't exactly see many faces back there anyway."

Nervously, Don Givens turned to exit the room. The cardiac surgeon had no real business hanging out in the Emergency Department, other than his wife had been called in to give an update on this particular patient. He thought it better not to spend too much more time in the room, people might start to ask questions. "You really were very lucky tonight, Billy. A man wielding a baseball bat could have done some serious, permanent damage."

"He could have done damage to any of us, doc. I suggest you be careful out there, too," Billy replied groggily.

CORA WASHINGTON, BEFORE HEADING TO HER SHIFT AT the gift shop, had explained to Allison that no one understood exactly what happened to Billy this evening, though Allison felt she had a pretty good idea. Now, after everyone else had vacated the dimly lit room, Allison, sitting next to Billy's bed, broke the silence, "I was worried to death when I got the call that you had been hurt. You could have been out there all alone lying on the concrete, no one there to help."

Billy looked at Allison. Gone was the bright smile, the blazing sense of humor, the sarcastic remarks. He took her hand, and with tears in his eyes responded, "You are the best friend that I have ever had, G.H. I feel like you were brought here for a reason."

Sadly, Allison believed that Billy considered her his best friend. It must have been torturous to grow up gay in a town like Noeware, Ga. The judgment, the taunting, the name calling — she just couldn't imagine. Squeezing his hand a little tighter, on the verge of tears herself, Allison said, "There is no judgment here Billy. You can let me know, even if it is by text, where you are going before you put yourself in a dangerous situation like that again. Someone should know where you are."

"You know, I lived in Atlanta once. I was only there for about six months. The ATL is the gay mecca for smalltown guys like me. You know that bar Blaine's? I lived right on Myrtle St. right behind it. I thought that I had arrived in a place perfect for me. You know what I mean?"

Allison knew exactly what he meant. A kid who was different, suddenly moving to a community filled with others like him. It must have been so validating. "Why did you only stay six months?"

"That place I thought was where I belonged made me feel like more of an outcast than Noeware, Ga ever could have. You must know Midtown Atlanta and what it's like? Well, the rent to live there cost every penny I figured out how to make. But the burbs didn't feel quite that safe. I couldn't even afford a good bike, much less a flashy car. I walked or rode the MARTA bus everywhere. I worked at a Denny's restaurant, so I couldn't afford to buy just the right clothes. Smelled like cigarettes and bacon grease half the time. I was too poor for the Midtown set, too country for the black gay community, too black for the white. I felt like I had fallen into a gaggle of middle school mean girls. And the whole time I felt like I could barely keep my head above water. It was awful. So, I gritted my teeth for six months to finish out my lease, kissed my security deposit goodbye, and got a bus ticket back to the familiar territory of Tennyson County. I have experienced a lot of things in this town Allison, both good and bad, but I have never been afraid here, not as an adult. That skinhead was out for blood. He wanted to kill me," Billy said as he burst into free-flowing tears. Allison leaned over and held him, for lack of knowing anything else that she could do to help. She comforted him for the better part of half an hour, realizing that she had never experienced such vulnerability with another human being before. Billy Washington may very well be her best friend, too.

"You were bullied as a child, weren't you?" Allison asked carefully.

Billy, nodding through his tears, was unable to conjure up a verbal answer.

"That must have been awful. Kids can be cruel, but I am so glad you had a loving and understanding family."

Finally able to catch enough breath to form words, Billy replied, "the worst of the bullying didn't stop until well after school."

Astonished, Allison stared at Billy wide-eyed, "You were bullied as an adult? What the hell? I can't believe that the police, or even your family, didn't put a stop to it."

"Well, G.H., the bully WAS family. I suppose one day you'll meet my brother, Carl Jr."

Due to a combination of strong pain medications and exhaustion, both of the physical and mental kind, Billy finally drifted off to sleep. His demeanor was so peaceful now, Allison knew that it was time to take her leave. With one last squeeze of his hand, Allison let go and headed for the corridor. The dim lighting of the hospital this time of night struck her as creepy, and she shuddered a bit thinking of every horror flick that she had ever seen. Laughing at her own silliness, she almost jumped through the water-stained drop tile ceiling when a hand touched her shoulder from behind. Turning quickly, though afraid of what she might see, she jerked a few feet away from where she had been standing.

Looking a little startled herself, Dr. Meg Givens exclaimed, "Oh Gosh, Ms. Edwards, I didn't mean to frighten you. I am so sorry."

"Oh, think nothing of it, I guess I am just a bit on edge," Allison replied as the goosebumps that had just taken over every square inch of the surface of her body started to recede.

"I'm about to head back home for the evening, but I am glad that I caught you."

"Oh no, is there something going on with Billy that we don't already know about?"

"Oh, no no no, he is actually in remarkable shape for someone who has been through what he has. With the relatively minor wounds that he has, I don't expect that the insurance company will want him to stay at the Hotel Tennyson

General for much more than a night," Meg Givens said, shaking her head at the bureaucracy that was today's healthcare system.

"That's actually great news, but then what did you want to see me about?"

"Well, I realize that this is going to come straight out of left field, and please do not feel any pressure, but I have an invitation for you. My sister Gail and I are getting together at her house tomorrow evening ...," looking at her watch, Meg corrected herself, "I suppose that's THIS evening. I was wondering if you'd like to join us for some wine and cheese, nothing formal. It's just that I know that you are writing a story about Noeware, and Gail and I have been here our entire lives and ..."

Allison interrupted her, as she had heard enough, "Yes, I'd love to. Most of the information that I have gathered has been supplied by one family, and while I have learned a lot, varied perspectives are needed for a great story."

"That's fantastic! I am just going to jot down my cell number for you," she said pulling out a small notepad from the chest pocket of her lab coat. "Just give me a call and I will give you directions. I'll be happy to send Hank to pick you up at the hotel and bring you over."

I'll be damned, Allison thought, Ole Hank is a real person. Grateful for the offer, but laughing to herself at the same time, she was convinced that Tennyson County resided directly in the center of *The Twilight Zone*.

PART THREE

Thursday, September 25
One Day Prior to the Murder

CHAPTER 10
NOEWARE, GA., THE FLOWER SHOP

The sun was bright, and the humidity hit early as Carol Wei turned the sign on the front door of the town's florist shop from closed to open. Her Attire for the day would seem completely inappropriate to anyone else, but her mauve sweater was necessary due to the shop's heavily air-conditioned environment. The Georgia sun would wilt her product in minutes if she didn't keep the thermostat somewhere between meat locker and crisper drawer temperature. She had just seen her daughter Daisy off to work at the Grand Hotel. Her husband Joe had left hours ago to sculpt the lawns of Tennyson County. She was just about to sit down for a final cup of morning coffee when someone entered the shop. With a quiet sigh, realizing her workday was beginning unusually early, she looked up with a smile.

"Good morning," Allison Edwards said, as she made her way past the cold cases filled with roses, carnations, daisies, and lilies. "I'm so sorry to make you get straight to work, but I was on my way to the hospital to see a friend, when I saw you turn the sign around. I was hoping to just grab a quick pre-made arrangement." Wearing a little more makeup than usual and dressed a little more professionally than she was used to, in slacks and a sleeveless blouse, Allison was prepared for a day full of meetings.

"Don't be silly," Carol replied, walking around her sales counter to meet Allison in the middle of the shop. For second generation Asian-Americans, her family had done very well in South Georgia. Her parents, a Chinese mother and American father, nearly worked themselves to death trying to provide for the family. They scrimped and saved every dime that they could to insure a better life for Carol. Carol and Joe in turn, tried their best to do the same for Daisy.

Reaching into a case beside where they were standing, Carol pulled out a vase holding peach roses and baby's breath, "Might this one be appropriate for the occasion?"

"Maybe something just a little more masculine," Allison responded while giggling to herself, feeling that masculinity and Billy Washington were oxymorons.

"Ahh, maybe something with a little more greenery? I think I have just the thing. Over by the window here, I just got in the largest African violets that I have ever seen. Do you think your friend would appreciate one of those?" The two made their way over to the violet display, and looked over, what Allison had to agree, was an amazing selection of plants.

"Perfect," Allison said as she grabbed a lovely potted plant with a deep purple bloom, "I think Billy will love this."

"Billy Washington?" Carol asked, looking closely at Allison's expression, "Billy Washington is in the hospital? Is everything okay?"

"Well, yes and no. He was attacked last night on his way home from work," Allison fibbed, as not to give up too much of Billy's personal business. "He has some relatively minor injuries, but he will probably be released today."

"I'm so sorry to hear about this," Carol said with genuine concern, "I hope you will give him my best. I'm Carol Wei by the way," the florist said offering her hand.

"Of course, I will," Allison replied as she returned the gesture, "I'm Allison Edwards."

"Oh, you are the young lady writing the story on Noeware, aren't you?"

"That's me," Allison replied, feeling like the most unlikely celebrity ever.

"Let's get you checked out," Carol said walking back behind the sales desk, "But I will be honest with you, I'd go with the roses for Billy."

"Sold," Allison said with a huge grin, knowing that the florist was exactly right.

OUTSIDE THE FLOWER SHOP, ALLISON PULLED OUT HER phone to call Jess. She had gotten so caught up in her visit to Noeware, time had escaped her. She nodded a quick hello to Miss Willa, who was walking by and pulling her suitcase. Miss Willa lit up, smiled back, but kept walking as if she was on a mission. Allison was really enamored with this place, but she was jolted back to reality when Jess answered her call.

"Hey, you," Jess said, through lots of background noise.

"Hey there. Everything going well at home?"

"Sure, although I feel like I have done nothing but work since you've been gone. You know how it is at the CDC, meetings about meetings. Oh, I did stop into your shop this morning, just to kind of check on things. You'll be happy to know that Dennis took your advice and dumped that girl who was only using him for his free weekly pound of coffee."

Laughing and shaking her head, Allison responded, "Well, that was bound to happen sooner rather than later. I hope he let her down easy; she has become dependent on that caffeine."

"Huh? Oh yeah, I think all is well. Sorry, just a little distracted, three things going at once."

"Understood. I'll let you go. I have a very busy day here, myself."

"Talk later, honey. I am so glad that you are having fun."

Allison disconnected the call, feeling bummed. She didn't get a chance to update Jess on anything that had happened over the past few days, and so much had happened. Between Billy's attack, dinner with the Washingtons, meeting with the mayor, being followed …

"Damn it," Allison exclaimed as she remembered that she still had to file a report with Chief Thomas, though she didn't really know why, he didn't seem convinced that she had been followed in the first place. She decided that she would stop by the police department, which was located just a floor below the mayor's office, right after she visited Billy at the hospital.

Today's schedule was already filling up, and it wasn't even 10a.m.

Glancing down the street, Allison saw Miss Willa sitting on a bench mumbling to herself. She made a mental note to try to catch up with the woman at some point over the next 24 hours, as she may very well be able to provide an interesting perspective about the town from a very different point of view.

IN THE DISTANCE, THE G.R.I.T. ANNOUNCED ITS morning arrival.

Wooooooooooooot

CHAPTER 11
TENNYSON COUNTY, WADDELL RESIDENCE

An ancient bloodhound grabbed the last bit of shade available under an old, dilapidated Ford pickup truck sitting next to an even more dilapidated single-wide mobile home. Its dirt front yard adorned by the occasional weed, old used tire, and car parts. One would think the scene was straight out of the depression era, if it weren't for the well-kept modern houses dotting the highway leading to it. The owners of said modern houses complained regularly to the county commission about the state of the Waddell property.

Inside, Jeremiah Waddell sat in his recliner drinking a canned beer, though the clock was still showing that lunchtime was more than an hour away. His right hand missing, replaced by a stump, was in his lap. The television remote was in his left hand. "Don't buy a vowel, you twit," he yelled at the out of place, large flat screen television, just before shutting it off as his son Cash entered the room. "What in hell did the cops want with you out in the yard earlier?" he asked. "I told you not to bring trouble home, boy."

"Somebody went and jumped that Billy Washington last night downtown. They were trying to say that I had something to do with it."

Standing, becoming red-faced, Jeremiah put his own face within inches of his son's, "Ruth's nephew? THAT Billy Washington? And did you have anything to do with it?"

"Nah, you sound just like the cops. I was doing that job for you last night, remember?"

"What have I always told you?", the old man asked while raising his voice, "You do not mess with Ruthless. There is nothing that woman wouldn't do to see every member of this family rot in prison. If she can't pin something on us, she'd lie to get a conviction anyway."

"I told you; I didn't have nuthin' to do with it. I am getting about sick and tired of being caught in the middle of YOUR history with that woman."

Cash could barely get the words out of his mouth, before his father backhanded him across the face, leaving his ear ringing.

Cash turned and looked directly into his father's eyes. In a level tone of voice, he said "Old Man, you may not have noticed I have 30 pounds and five inches on you. And both my working arms. You lay a hand on me like that again, I'll bury you alive under one of the old cars in the backyard."

Realizing that his son meant what he was saying, Jeremiah added a few feet of distance between himself and Cash. No matter how often and bitterly the two clashed, they needed each other. Their less than reputable business depended on both men to stay involved, Jeremiah for his contacts, Cash as the strongman. Though Jeremiah realized that he was becoming less vital to the business the older he got, as Cash was making many contacts of his own. He had to make sure that there were things that he, and only he, knew about the business, so that his participation remained imperative.

"Look, all I am saying is this, only break the law one way at a time," Jeremiah continued. "That's a lesson my daddy taught me when I was younger than you. We don't need the cops showin' up out here for one thing then discovering another. Understand?"

"I'm not going to tell you again; I didn't do anything to that… boy."

"Lord help me; I believe you. Let's just keep it that way."

Neither man noticed the set of small eyes peeping around the corner from the hall. Little Annie Waddell, soon to be four years old, was becoming accustomed to witnessing family scenes such as this. She couldn't make sense of everything they said, but she had grown adept at reading faces. Her mother was a meth addict who had simply disappeared one day, when Annie was about two. Thankfully, she was past weaning age and almost out of diapers, or the Waddell men might have turned Annie over to the state. But as it was, everyone, Cash included, figured Misti Waddell had run off, and they didn't feel like inviting the scrutiny of DFACS – what the people of Noeware called DFCS, the Georgia Division of Family and Children Services. The Waddell men had tolerated the toddler and kept her mostly fed and clean, with the sometimes help of either man's flavor of the week, most of whom doted on Annie for however long they hung around.

Now, she turned back towards the room with her bed – she shared it with boxes of what her paw called "inventory" — only breaking into a scamper after she knew her kin couldn't see her. Not that they were watching her, but you never knew when they might find it convenient to take notice. Once she was in her room, she dove onto her bed and pulled the covers over her head then held her breath under the covers until her lungs nearly burst, craving oxygen. This was part of her ritual, too: Hold her breath as long as she could, until the searing in her chest overrode the pain in her heart. One time, she thought she had really passed out. Maybe one day she could hold it and never breathe in again.

OUTSIDE IN THE YARD, CASH ATTEMPTED TO SIT ON THE metal hood of the old Ford, before realizing that it was scorching. He leaned against it instead, pulling out the burner phone that he had been supplied with a week ago. After a few rings, there was an answer on the other end and Cash spoke.

"The nazi did the job that you wanted done. I'll keep you posted on the rest." Without waiting for a reply, he disconnected.

CHAPTER 12
NOEWARE, GA., POLICE DEPARTMENT

"Chief, Allison Edwards is here to see you," Detective Abernathy said as he passed the open office door. There was a lot of activity afoot in the station, as the town was preparing for Founders' Day activities. The police department wasn't just responsible for the day's security, but it also had a float of its own for the traditional parade. There was a lot to do, so Chief Ernie Thomas had little time nor patience for a "might have been followed" — situation. However, this matter was one more thing that had been added to his to-do list, and he was eager to check it off.

Waving Allison into his office, the chief got straight down to business.

"Well, Ms. Edwards, I appreciate you finally taking a moment out of your busy schedule to sit down with me."

"I appreciate you making time for me Chief Thomas, although I don't think that my particular situation has been much of a priority for you."

"On the contrary, Ms. Edwards," the chief said smiling, "I am always available to investigate any actual crimes that take place in this city."

"Actual crimes? Actual crimes? I can't help but notice that, and not for the first time this week, Chief Thomas, you have suggested that my being followed was all in my head."

"Well, allegedly being followed isn't necessarily a crime in Noeware, but I am happy to hear you out."

Exasperated, Allison sighed heavily and continued, "As I have told you before, Chief, I felt like someone was following me from the moment I left the hotel the other night."

"Felt like someone was following you, or saw someone follow you?", the chief interrupted.

"Well, I didn't exactly see anyone."

"Let me write this down, alleged victim of a possible crime, saw no one following her."

"If I am here to be ridiculed Chief Thomas, I fear that we are both wasting our time. I did not choose to come in to make a statement, I am here at your insistence. I have many, many more important matters that I could be attending to, if this incident is not something that you are going to take seriously."

Intrigued by the woman's spunk, Chief Thomas couldn't control his grin, "The way I see it, young lady, there is no proof of any incident at all, only a feeling that someone from the big city had, while walking around an unfamiliar small town alone at night — while drinking."

"This is not the first time that you have brought up alcohol consumption, sir. For the record, I resent the hell out of it. I had A drink, as in one, and was overcome by the heat, humidity, and possible stalking."

"Ahhhh, so you now admit that the stalking may have never happened?"

"Why exactly am I here, Chief Thomas? Do you not have any litterbugs or jaywalkers to harass this morning?"

Now in a full on fit of laughter, respecting the woman's ability to go toe to toe with him, Chief Thomas replied, "You are a fiery one, I will give you that, Ms. Edwards. I just don't think that we have enough to go on in order to suspect that a crime was committed."

"Fiery? Are you kidding me right now? Chief Thomas, I am doing my level best to remain respectful to you as a person, as well as to your position in this community, but I will not have you patronize me again! If you think there is no evidence of a crime, I am happy to accept your professional opinion, but I'll be damned if I am going to sit here and have you pat me on the head like a little girl who just dropped her ice cream cone." Standing to leave, Allison leaned over the desk of the police chief until she was looking directly into his eyes, "Here me clearly, Chief Thomas, when anyone, male or female, walks into this office with a situation that he or she takes seriously, the very least you could do is pretend to take the matter seriously yourself. You might want to try being a little more of a public servant and a little less of a horse's ass."

With that, Allison stormed out of the office, through a gaggle of uniformed officers who had obviously been eavesdropping on her conversation with the chief, and out the front door. In the corridor she pressed the down button on the elevator … repeatedly.

Back in his office, Chief Ernie Thomas had a permanent smile plastered on his face, as he appeared to be in deep thought. Detective Abernathy stepped back into the office shaking his head, "Chief, I think you may have met your match."

"Ha, I think I'd like to know a little more about that woman."

"Well, I hate to drag you out of Fantasyland, chief, but Patrice is on line two, and she doesn't sound very happy."

"She never does, Abernathy, she never does," he replied while answering his ex-wife's call.

CHAPTER 13
NOEWARE, GA., THE G.R.I.T. DEPOT

To many, the sight of an old man painting on canvas in the passenger car of a stationary train might seem bizarre, but in Noeware, Ga., it just meant that R.W. was at work. The man, always dressed in pinstriped blue and white overalls with matching hat, had been working the G.R.I.T. for as long as anyone could remember. His days of engineering the train himself were long gone, but his guidance to the current train operator, as well as his counsel to the people of the town at large, were roles that he wouldn't soon be letting go of. He was a fixture in Noeware, and this morning he had an early visitor, if not an unexpected one.

As she approached the train car, a to-go coffee in her hand, R.W. reached out to assist her in climbing aboard. Quickly, he changed his mind as she cut her eyes at him as if in warning. With considerable effort, she climbed the steep, steel steps, leaving her walker behind, and sat in the row of seats behind her old friend. Visits like this were commonplace between the two town elders going back decades. This morning, Ruth was troubled. This morning was not unusual.

R.W. spoke first as the mayor got comfortable on the bench, "Well, good morning, Mayor Blakely, to whom do I owe the honor of this visit?"

"I think that we can dispense with the formalities, Picasso, we are way past any pretenses here, you and I."

"Fair enough my friend; what's on your mind," he asked as he focused his visual attention on the painting in progress but listened attentively to his guest.

Though the angle of the canvas prohibited Ruth from seeing the emerging image, she could guess what the subject matter was. R.W. was an observer of both people and places. There were few who had ever crossed the border of Tennyson County who had escaped his paint brush. Ruth imagined that his house must look like a shrine to decades of residents and visitors who had moved in and out of their lives, a virtual museum of life stories.

"I suppose you know that the girl from Atlanta arrived a few days ago?"

"Well, I reckon I did hear something about that, yes."

"It seems that she and William have become quite fond of each other. I can't say that I saw that coming."

"Well now, I bet you didn't, but I have a feelin' that you ain't here to talk to me about a buddin' friendship between your nephew and …"

"No, you're right, as usual." Looking down at her feet, because she felt unable to make eye contact, Ruth continued, "We had a meeting. She asked about the town's history. She even asked me about Cora, Carl, and the rest. I brushed it off.

I got a little carried away with my storytelling. My emotions had been building all morning, after an early meeting with that Cash Waddell."

"I take it that meetin' didn't end happily?"

Ruth rolled her eyes by way of answering him, "I suppose that I've been a bit passionate this week."

"Hurt people hurt people, Ruthie," R.W. replied while still looking at his artwork, rather than the mayor. "You and I both know why the girl is here. I recommend that you have a sit down with her. I believe that she'll be a lot more understandin' than you give her credit for. Besides, how long do you think it is going to take Carl to slip up and tell her that the journalism grant that she was awarded is bogus, and that the money was fronted by you?"

"As much as I hate to admit it, you're right. I think it would be best if she heard everything from me, rather than getting bits and pieces through her interviews with others."

"Now you are seeing things clearly my dear friend," R.W. replied, as the familiar orange tabby rubbed lovingly around his ankle, purring at high volume. "Well, good mornin' to you Miss Dewie."

Glancing down at the cat, Ruth said, "you know, there's something just not right about a cat that doesn't meow."

"Now, I don't reckon that's a whole lot stranger than a woman who don't feel, do you?"

Raising an eyebrow at the man, Ruth resisted the urge to argue, responding simply with, "touché."

R.W. rubbed his lower back, a holdover ache from an old injury, as he made direct eye contact with the mayor, "You know what you are Ruthie? You are what folks call an enigmatic paradox."

"Ha, no folks around here would say that. Most couldn't spell it. Go on, I'm listening."

"You're a bit of a mystery — a contradiction. You come off as a structure cold enough to sink the titanic, but you have the biggest heart I reckon I've ever seen.

"Maybe you aren't as familiar with me as you think, old man."

"Well, there ain't nobody in this county that knows you better, the good, bad, and ugly. Now, if there's nothing else, I think it's about time we get this ole girl ready to move for the day," R.W. said while giving the train a once over, "unless you are finally ready to …"

Ruth stood, using the back of the train seat to assist her. As she slowly climbed back down the steps, she looked over her shoulder and said, while completely cutting off her friend, "very eye-opening chat R.W. I don't know what I would do without you."

"One day you'll have to figure that out Ruthie, but I don't reckon that day'll be comin' too soon."

As Mayor Ruth Blakely grabbed her walker and proceeded towards Main Street and away from the train depot, R.W. watched her exit. He smiled at their shared history, delighted that she still sought solace in their conversations. As she disappeared from view, he glanced back at his current painting with a concerned look. He sighed deeply as he placed his initials in the bottom right corner. Taking the painting in, he approved of his work, but fretted over the image of a man with a shaved head, that he had never seen before.

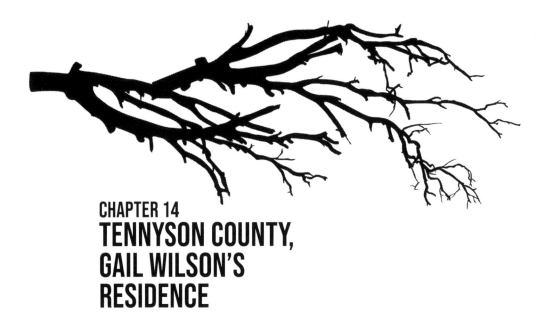

CHAPTER 14
TENNYSON COUNTY, GAIL WILSON'S RESIDENCE

The day had passed quickly, as Allison Edwards had interviewed a half dozen prominent (and not so prominent) citizens of Noeware. She felt as if she was really getting a feel for the town she had only known as the butt of jokes a few days ago. There was a rich history here, an old south meets new in a somewhat confusing mash-up of personalities and stereotypes. She was beginning to develop a lot of respect for the hurdles that one must jump in order to rise above his/her historical standing. In a lot of cases, it couldn't have been easy.

Now, taking in the view of Scenic Highway from the passenger side of Hank Johnson's army green pickup truck, she still couldn't believe that Ole Hank was for real. She caught her first view of a suburban part of the county that she hadn't seen before. A subdivision emerged on her right, full of one-story brick houses, mostly identical to each other, differentiated only by the color of their faux wooden shutters and trim.

She'd date the subdivision from around the 1950s. True to a neighborhood well into its seventh decade, a handful of the homes were showing their age, but most had gotten face-lifts (mostly well done, but not a few cheap renovations thrown in as well).

Gail Wilson lived alone in the third house on the left past the turn onto Dahlia Blossom Lane. It was, of course, one of the higher-quality updates, to a home that had had more bells and whistles than its neighbors in the first place. The landscaping was artistic and immaculate at the same time.

Gail and her sister Meg had requested an early get together, as Meg and her husband Don had a prior engagement later in the evening. Allison assumed that it was a hospital function, as the two doctors were known by everyone in town to be serious workaholics. Billy had been completely jealous of the invitation that Allison had received for wine and cheese at Gail's house. However, he was satisfied by the promise that he would be filled in later on all of the tawdry details, though Allison had no reason to believe that there would be anything scandalous revealed at all.

Thanking Hank and tipping him generously as the truck came to a stop in Gail's driveway, Allison made her way to the front door. The doorbell had barely finished chiming when Gail Wilson opened the door and held out her hand, "Allison Edwards, thank you so much for coming. It's a pleasure to welcome you to my home."

Allison could see that Gail's people skills didn't end when she clocked out from her position at the hotel, and Allison felt like she was already well acquainted with the woman from seeing her repeatedly as she passed through the lobby. "I appreciate you having me. It's not every day that a woman gets to have cheese and wine with descendants of one of the founding fathers of Tennyson County."

Dr. Meg Givens, who had joined her sister at the door, laughed at the absurdity of what Allison had just said, though every word was true. "Come on in, refreshments are already set out on the island in the kitchen."

The house was much more spacious than it appeared from outside, more modern in appearance as well. While Gail Wilson was dressed more casually in khakis, tucked in baby blue pocket t-shirt and loafers, her sister was wearing slacks, a short-sleeved black cotton blouse and heels. It was obvious that this meeting was only a precursor to the rest of Meg's night. The three ladies took their places on bar stools in the kitchen around the island, where a bottle of red wine was breathing, a platter of various gourmet cheeses was featured, and two stemmed wine glasses were available.

"Oh, are you not drinking Dr. Givens? We didn't have to make this a wine and cheese chat if you needed to keep a clear head for your meeting later," Allison said.

"Oh, I'm drinking alright," Meg replied with a laugh, "It's Mother Superior over here that won't be partaking. Oh, and it's Meg, no more of this Dr. Givens stuff, and she's Gail, period."

"I've been sober for the past seven years, Allison. I am afraid that alcoholism runs in our family, but my sister never let that fact get in the way of a good bottle of wine," Gail added.

Allison was startled by the frankness of her hostess, but it allowed her to let her guard down a little and become more comfortable with the two women. Meg poured wine for Allison first, then herself, and the three women settled in for a little conversation.

As small talk was ending, and the second bottle of wine was opened, the topic of conversation became a little more serious. Allison suddenly got the distinct feeling that there was an agenda afoot that she had previously been unaware of. She felt like things were about to get a whole lot more interesting.

"Well, I think it's confession time," Gail said, refilling her orange juice glass and topping it off with a little club soda.

"Here we go," her sister chimed in, preparing herself for some potential awkwardness.

"Allison, I hope that what I am about to tell you doesn't send you packing, or make you think less of Meg and me. I like you. I can tell that my sister does too, so I want to be completely straight with you. Deception is no way to start off a potential friendship."

Allison braced herself for a bombshell, "I'm all ears."

"You might have noticed the large number of reporters staying at the hotel. That is not a coincidence. Founders' Day is right around the corner, and the vultures have gathered in town with the expectation that our daddy, Harrison Tennyson, will use the occasion to announce a U.S. Senate bid."

"Oh," Allison replied, receiving the answer to one of the

questions that had been plaguing her for the past few days. "I'll admit, I did wonder why the press was here in such large numbers."

"The unfortunate thing about the press, is that they are always looking for something besides the obvious. While they are all here hoping for an announcement, they dig for dirt in the meantime. Let's face it, Noeware isn't exactly hopping with entertainment possibilities, so while the reporters are here and bored, they try to make news, instead of just cover it. Does that make any sense at all?"

"Actually, it makes a lot of sense to me, and it is a pretty good reminder to this journalism student, not to get caught up in an attempt to do the same."

Gail nodded, took a deep breath, exhaled and continued, "Here is where the confession comes in. Meg and I read the story about you in the Noeware Journal, the one about you receiving the grant to write your story. We really liked what we read, thought you did a lovely job with the story on Anniston, and had an idea. What if we could convince you to write a human-interest story on daddy? You would get an interview that none of the other reporters would have, it would be great for daddy's campaign, and in turn would be a boost to your career."

"Oh wow," Allison exclaimed, genuinely surprised by this revelation. "I must say, I am certainly flattered by all of this, but I am not sure that I have the experience."

Meg, tipsy from the wine, cut Allison off mid-sentence to say, "we know that you have the experience. What my sister is leaving out is this, our mother volunteered to use a private investigator friend in Atlanta to do some digging on you and your work. We have read nearly everything that you have written in the last few years, from basic news writing to fluff pieces on turtle spawning at Piedmont Park. We think you are exactly the person to write daddy's story, if you are willing to do so now that you know what we have been up to."

Now, Allison was in shock. The women that she was enjoying wine with had used a private investigator to spy on her. She took a few moments to gather herself before saying, "I won't lie, I don't really have the words to appropriately react to what you both have just told me. So, Jessica …"

"We know all about Jessica," Gail replied.

"Oh my God, that is why you referenced her the night that I checked into the hotel."

"I have been wondering for days if you caught that little slip up. I am so sorry that we haven't been honest with you before now, but I hope you'll understand that this was really our first opportunity. Please do not feel obligated at all to take us up on the offer of the interview, we just felt it was important to let you know what we had been up to."

"Your father, is he really about to make an announcement that he is running for senate?"

"He will be making an announcement. He has been planning this for years, but he isn't going to be doing it during the Founders' Day festivities. I am afraid that the press is barking up the right tree, at the wrong time."

"How about this," Allison started, still trying to collect herself, "I will give the exclusive interview some thought, if we can change the subject for the rest of the evening and get to know each other better. Does that sound fair?"

"More than fair," Meg agreed. "Gail, would you mind

making a pot of coffee? This is going to be a long evening for me, and it wouldn't be a good idea for me to have any more of this wine, as delicious as it is."

Gail nodded and turned to start the coffee making process. Meg got up to start clearing up the cheese platter and wine glasses. Allison offered to help but was turned down by both women.

Allison had to admit to herself that the women really did tell her the truth at the first opportunity. It's not like any of them had had the chance for a lengthy conversation prior to tonight. They certainly had no intention of using anything that they found out about her against her, not that there was much controversial information there to begin with. She was sure that she could accept that this happened, understand that the women were just being protective of their father, and continue getting acquainted with them. Allison had never known her own father, her mother becoming pregnant as the result of a casual encounter, but she felt closer to the sisters having caught a glimpse of the fierce affection that they had for their dad. She was a little envious.

"How about since we are being honest, I ask some questions that have been on my mind, and you ladies help me out a little?"

"Oh goodie, hit us with your best shot," Meg responded.

"I'd say it is the least we could do," Gail agreed.

"Okay, tell me about your thoughts on Ruth Blakely."

"Well …," Gail started.

"Racist!" Meg interrupted, then clapped her hands over her mouth, aware that a daughter of the family the county was named after calling a black woman racist would appear every bit as terrible as it was. The wine had brought out more honesty than she'd planned. But Allison noted that she didn't contradict herself.

"Racist? Are you serious, Meg? I was going to say impressive," Gail chastised. "By all accounts, the woman has been through a lot. Hell, she looks like every step she takes is excruciating. You couldn't pay me to walk a mile in her shoes."

"Miss Willa," Allison threw out, just to see if the ladies were familiar with the woman at all.

"Pitiful," Gail answered first this time.

"Now there's a woman whose shoes I wouldn't want to walk in," Meg added.

"I am assuming that she's homeless?"

"Homeless? Oh Lord no," Gail answered with a laugh. "Willa Banks lives in the Manager's Suite built behind the front desk of the Grand Hotel. She's not homeless, she lives like a queen."

Astonished, Allison followed up, "She does? How in the world does she afford such a thing?"

"Saint Ned pays for it every month," Meg answered, cutting her eyes at her sister.

"Ned Wilson? Your ex-husband Ned? The Ned that owns the diner?" Allison directed the questions to Gail, while making a mental note to investigate why Ned Wilson would do such a thing.

"The one and the same," Gail said, lowering her eyes as if ashamed. "I never said that he wasn't the nicest man in Tennyson County."

"Pardon me for asking, and just say so if this is none of my business …"

"Why would I divorce the nicest man in Tennyson County? Oh, you may ask, you aren't the first. Because, I haven't been the nicest woman in Tennyson County. When I was drinking, I put that poor man through a living hell, and no man should have had to deal with that version of me."

"He is the absolute love of her life," Meg said shaking her head. "We have all tried to convince Gail to stop punishing herself for the sins of the past, but that is the way of the world for folks around here. Ned would remarry her tomorrow if she said yes, but her guilt won't let her receive his love. It's tragic, really. She loves the man so much, that she will spend the rest of her life protecting him from the woman she no longer is."

Allison was touched by the power of what Meg had just said. She didn't think she could fathom a love that strong. How did it not eat Gail alive to see the love of her life every single day, but not be with him because she was afraid to hurt him? Tragic didn't begin to describe it. Allison was blown away.

"How about your mother," Allison asked, in hopes of changing a very difficult subject.

"Well, that's Camille," Gail responded, appearing relieved to talk about something else, even if it was her mother. "She has been splitting her time between New York and Washington D.C. for the past few months, doing some fundraising and preliminary work for daddy's campaign."

"Let's just say that mother is an enormous fish in the miniscule pond that is Tennyson County," Meg explained. "If there is an opportunity to escape, she'll take it. Now, speaking of escaping …" Meg glanced at her watch, "I am afraid that I must go, or I am going to be late for my meeting. I really hate to run; this has been fun."

Gail walked her sister out to her car, while Allison sipped on her coffee. Once they were standing next to the Mercedes, Gail asked, "are you going to be okay to drive? I'll be happy to call Hank."

"Oh, I'm fine. I actually didn't have nearly as much wine as it appears that I did; I let Allison down it in hopes of softening the blow of our little truth telling."

"If you're sure."

"Positive."

"One more thing …"

"No Gail. Don't you dare tell her. It's none of our business."

"But …"

"But nothing! Some things one must discover on her own. Besides, how do we know that she doesn't already know?"

"Maybe you're right."

"Trust me, I am."

As Gail turned to leave, she had one more question, "you really think Ruth is racist? I had no idea that you felt that way about her."

"Seriously, you have to ask? Have you not seen the way that she treats daddy?"

"Funny, I always thought daddy was the racist."

CHAPTER 15
NOEWARE, GA., RUTH'S CONDOMINIUM

In the top floor flat of the three-story building separating the Grand Hotel from the eyesore that is the Tennyson General Hospital, Ruth Blakely, wearing only a red silk robe, stared into a mirror affixed to the top of her bureau. Brushing the gray hair that she painstakingly straightened daily, she spoke without turning around, "I don't care how many times he denies it, there is no doubt in my mind that Cash Waddell is responsible for what happened to William. It was complete retribution for my having had words with him earlier that morning."

Turning over in the bed to face her, keeping his naked body mostly covered by the white cotton sheet, Harrison Tennyson replied, "Look Ruthie, you wanted the police to question him, and they did, even though the description that Billy gave to Ernie Thomas in no way matched Cash Waddell. I am not denying that the man is involved in a lot of unscrupulous things, but I really don't think he had anything to do with this."

"I'm telling you he did! If not directly, he knows more about what happened than he is letting on. The assault happened within the city limits; I'll have Ernie stay on this until the truth is uncovered. We just don't have violence of this sort on a regular basis. This is far too coincidental. I don't know why you put up with that family's bumbling mischief anyway."

"I've told you before, they are useful idiots. Often, they give away the farm with regards to information when being questioned, and it helps us clear our desks of petty crime cases. The fact that we gained zero information during this particular interrogation, makes me certain that Cash is innocent of this."

"Don't you ever use the name Cash Waddell and the word innocent in the same sentence with me. If that is your honest opinion, you are more foolish than I thought, and you are not a foolish man, Harry Tennyson. I better not find out that you are keeping anything important from me."

"In my life, I have never kept anything important from you, Ruthie, but we both know that the same can't be said for you."

Stung by Harrison's blow, Ruth replied, "Well, on that note, I think it's about time you left. You'll need to be extra quiet leaving; William is resting in his apartment downstairs. Thank God he's home, that damned cat of his moaned nearly the entire time he was in the hospital."

Harry sat up on the side of the bed and began to gather his clothes. Looking at Ruth as he dressed, he had said with a tortured look, "I really am very sorry that this happened, but it could have been so much worse. I think, all said, he got off pretty lucky."

With rage in her eyes, and a newfound flush on her cheeks, Ruth turned and spit out, "Don't give me that, 'He got off lucky' garbage, Harry. You and I both know that this happened because of who he is, not because of something that he's done. No one 'gets off lucky' after having been beaten simply for being different. That is something that a Tennyson will never understand. None of you have ever been **different** in any way. Your problem has always been, you confuse sympathy with empathy. You act like you understand the issues that the common man deals with day in and day out, but the truth is, you were born on third base and think you hit a triple. It's okay sometimes to admit that you don't understand some things. Acknowledgement of ignorance on a particular subject can make you seem more human. A willingness to learn from that ignorance can make you a better senator. People recognize disingenuous empathy, but they respect well placed sympathy."

"I don't think you've ever referred to me as 'senator' before, Ruthie. You really expect me to win the race?"

"This is exactly what I am talking about Harry. We are having a conversation about someone being the victim of a hate crime, and all you heard me say is 'you will make a good senator'. I would suggest that such self-centeredness wouldn't play well in a political campaign, except that lately it appears to be exactly what the voting public is looking for. Congratulations, you are well on your way to victory."

Harrison looked over at Ruth as she tucked her freshly

brushed hair into a silk bonnet. "There's the cap again, I will never understand black women."

Looking straight into his reflection in her mirror, rather than turning to face him, Ruth replied, "Why they gotta be black? I'd venture to say that you don't understand women — period. If you did, you would have never married Camille Archer to begin with."

Completely dressed now and turning the knob to step onto the hallway landing, Harry bid Ruth a goodnight, as he had no response to her comment. She was exactly right; they both knew it.

"The coffeehouse downstairs closed early tonight, so you won't have to worry about anyone seeing you pass by there but remember what I said about William. Close the ground floor door quietly," Ruth said as she carefully straightened the bonnet. "Oh, give Camille my love when you speak with her," Ruth finished grinning like a Cheshire cat.

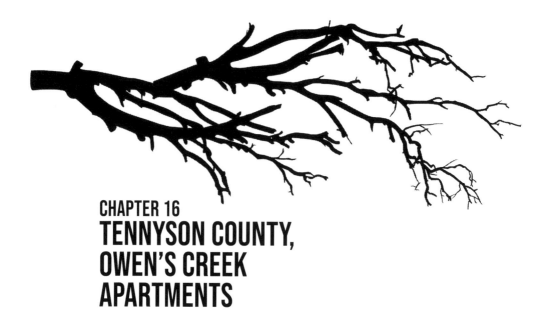

CHAPTER 16
TENNYSON COUNTY, OWEN'S CREEK APARTMENTS

Tennyson County was home to a few modern apartment developments. Only a few were needed, as the county wasn't exactly a flourishing hub of enterprise. Most of the residents of the apartments worked in factories on the edge of town, or in the healthcare industry. The beige stucco-sided apartments were well kept and priced moderately to make them a good choice for middle income renters. They stood in near solitude behind a gated entrance near what used to be, for generations, a secluded walking path, overlooking a creek whose flowing water held many Tennyson County secrets.

Tonight, though it was getting late, Doctors Don and Meg Givens were finishing up their glasses of wine, as well as their covert meeting with hospital nurse Patricia Barfield, R.N. The long planned get together was scheduled late purposely, as none of the three participants were eager for anyone at the hospital to know that they were seeing each other socially.

There was no reason to stir up the smalltown rumor mill with speculation, until a deal was reached, and papers were signed. Tonight, the hope was to seal said deal.

Carrying his wine glass to the sink to rinse it, despite the protests of his hostess, Don Givens asked, "So, we are all in agreement? This is actually going to happen?"

With tears forming in her eyes, his wife Meg looking anxiously at Patricia, "Are you saying yes, for real?"

"It sure looks like it," the nurse responded, though some uncertainty remained in her voice.

"Don't misunderstand," Meg added, "we aren't trying to convince you to do anything that you aren't positive is going to work for you. I won't have the papers drawn up if you have any trepidation whatsoever."

"No, I'm in, let's do it."

Meg threw her arms around the nurse, as Don, a grin on his face, joined them in the small living room. "Fantastic!", he said taking his turn in the hug line when his wife was finished.

"We will speak with our attorney about completing the paperwork to get the ball rolling. This is great news for all of us Patricia; you have no idea how much this means to Don and me."

After saying their goodnights and leaving the apartment, the two doctors sat quietly for a moment in their car. The sheer importance of what had just happened was overwhelming to them both. Finally, Meg spoke first …

"We are going to have a baby, Don."

"Well, we at least have the possibility of having a baby, Meg. Let's not get too far ahead of ourselves."

"Can't you just give me a few seconds to be excited, before

you bring up all of the technicalities, all of which I am already well aware of?"

"I'm sorry, you're right. I must remind myself sometimes to feel like a man, instead of thinking like a doctor. Holy Shit, we are going to have a baby!"

Laughing through tears, Meg placed her right hand lightly on her husband's left cheek, "There is no one I would rather raise a child with, Don Givens. You are going to be the best daddy."

INSIDE THE APARTMENT, PATRICIA OPENED ANOTHER bottle of wine. She had no idea how she had gotten herself into this predicament, or if there was a way that she could get herself out of it. Tipsy, she stood up from the sofa, and walked back to her bedroom. She knew that she had to get everything cleaned up before her roommate Rhonda Conner, a nurse in the hospital's Emergency Department, came home from work. The mess could wait a little longer she thought, as she turned on her bedroom's overhead light.

Opening her clothes closet, she reached for a boot box on the top shelf and placed it carefully on her bed. Removing the lid, she sat beside the box and pulled out the first news article. "Medical Resident Donald Givens Saves a Choking Woman in Grady Cafeteria," the headline exclaimed. "Tennyson General Welcomes Doctor Givens, Times Two," the next headline screamed. Article after article, in a well-organized pile, mentioned Don Givens in one way or another. Newspaper clippings that she had been collecting for years but kept hidden away to protect what had become an obsession.

She had gotten to know Donald Givens very well, before she had ever laid eyes on the man in person. She had collected announcements from every facet of his life: High school graduation, college graduation, engagement, residency, medical school. Patricia owned any and all media mention of Dr. Don Givens. She knew this hobby wasn't healthy, she couldn't help herself. Accepting a job in his department at the hospital named after his wife's family, now this seemed way over the line. She did it anyway.

For most of her adult life, Patricia had focused her attention on this man. He was a genius, a hero, a terrific athlete, until he realized that a sports injury wasn't something a surgeon should risk. However, what he had never been was a father. So, innocently enough, she asked him one day if he and Meg had ever thought about having children. To her surprise, he opened up completely, pouring out his emotions on the subject to a nurse he hadn't known for more than a few months. It was obvious that despite their failed attempts to conceive, Meg and Don desperately wanted to have a child of their own. Unfortunately for them, Meg was unable to carry a child to term. This, though now she realized how foolish it was, gave Patricia an opening.

She spent months making sure that she had the opportunity to speak to both doctors on a personal level — to get to know them well. She wanted them to see her as not just a coworker, but a trusted friend. Then one evening, an evening a lot like this one, she had the doctors over late at night for a visit. Instead of being direct, she talked around the subject of a baby so much, that Don and Meg thought she was suggesting a sexual threesome. Embarrassed, she clarified her intentions by way of making them an offer to be a surrogate, if they genuinely wanted to have a baby. These meetings went on periodically for months, culminating in tonight's finale.

"Now what," Patricia asked herself, still shuffling through decades worth of collected memorabilia. She didn't hate Meg Givens, but it was her husband that she was interested in. Not just interested in, fascinated by. She had used the ruse of surrogacy to draw the couple close, and now she felt stuck, like a mouse in a glue trap, unable to escape a situation of her own making. She wanted to make Don happy, and tonight he was happier than she had ever seen him before. The last thing she could face was disappointing him, she would die before she let that happen.

Patricia started to stand, as it really was time she cleaned up, but she was a little lightheaded from the wine. Rather than return the box to the closet, she tucked it under the bed. Maybe a short nap before cleaning wouldn't hurt anything. She closed her eyes, and with Dr. Don Givens on her mind, drifted off to sleep.

CHAPTER 17
MANHATTAN, NY., UPPER EAST SIDE

While the hour was very late in sleepy Tennyson County, Ga., the evening was just getting started in New York City, where Camille Tennyson had spent most of her time over the past eight months. She rented a stylish apartment in an affluent Upper East Side building, near the wealthiest of New Yorkers, gaining recognition and soliciting funds for a U.S. Senate campaign that would finally propel she and her husband Harrison from the town they were born and raised in, to the lifestyle she felt they so richly deserved.

This political race had been years in the making. The couple had both been born into wealthy and influential families, their union solidifying their stature in South Georgia. Harrison was soon elected to the Tennyson County Commission, and Camille had become his chief supporter and most trusted aide. It was a well-known fact that she wasn't the local bake sale type of political wife, she could roll her sleeves up and get her hands dirty with the politicians themselves. In fact, it was due to her own ambition, coupled with her desire to leave South Georgia behind, that she was able to convince her husband to make this senate run at all.

While Harry performed his day-to-day duties at home admirably, Camille spent months at a time schmoozing with the state's movers and shakers in Atlanta, Columbus, Athens, Savannah, and Augusta. Her charm and charisma had convinced state and local politicians throughout Georgia that Tennyson County could certainly be the home of their next senator. The work that she put in had resulted in 'Tennyson' becoming a household name in not just Georgia, but in the surrounding region. Harrison could give speeches in Birmingham, Charleston, Baton Rouge, just to name a few, and draw crowds reminiscent of a presidential candidate touring Iowa or New Hampshire. Of course, Camille was always by her husband's side at these events, and always took to the microphone herself at each rally to offer the red meat that fired up the crowd.

She knew that the time was coming soon for her to head back to Georgia, in order to be side by side with Harry when a public announcement was made. She was well on the path to having everything lined up for the event. With the help of Harry's sister Claire, she had teased the media outlets so well that they were already camping out at the Grand Hotel in Noeware waiting for the big day, even if Camille and Claire had been vague about when that day would be. The two women remained in daily communication, making sure that the anticipation and excitement level was maintained. Soon, the big payoff would happen — very soon.

Tonight, Camille was putting the finishing touches on her outfit for the final fundraiser in New York, before she left in the morning for Washington D.C., where there would be a few more fundraising meetings. Sliding on her new Jimmy Choo pumps, and spritzing herself with classic Miss Dior parfum, she headed for the door of the apartment. She checked her appearance in the mirror by the door one last time. Her Oscar de la Renta slacks and blouse were flawlessly appropriate for this event. They had been chosen specifically for Camille by her personal shopper at Bergdorf Goodman. This was the life that she and Harrison deserved. This is the life that they had earned.

Smiling at her new slightly longer than shoulder length hairstyle that had just been acquired this afternoon, grabbing her Alexander McQueen clutch purse with her freshly manicured hand, turning off the light in the apartment, she stepped into the hallway as the cellphone in the ridiculously expensive purse rang. Pausing, she felt for the device and checked the screen to see who was calling. Satisfied that it wasn't important, as no call from South Georgia would be important at that very moment, let alone one from her sister-in-law, Claire Montgomery, she silenced the phone and returned it to her purse. She'd return Claire's call later. Her husband's sister was useful, but she wasn't an ally. Camille and Claire were adversaries, but adversaries who currently needed each other.

The elevator ride down to the lobby was quick, stopping only once for another occupant, who like Camille nodded a greeting, but remained silent for the rest of the ride. Outside, a limousine had been arranged by the building's concierge to pick her up and take her to the party. The driver greeted her warmly while opening the door for her. Alone in the backseat, she reminded herself again that this, not peanut and tobacco farming, is what her future looked like.

About six blocks away, the car pulled over to the sidewalk, where a few awaiting members of the press clamored to take pictures of her arrival. They were tipped off by Camille herself, of course. All smiles and pageant waves, she walked towards the door being held open by the doorman. Once inside, she popped a small mint in her mouth, checked her teeth for lipstick with her compact, and entered the hotel banquet room.

"Well, how are y'all?" she asked while shaking every hand in sight. "It's so good to see y'all," she continued, laying her South Georgia accent on thick. "Thanks for coming darlin'." Her arrival made her the center of attention, exactly how she expected things to be when she and Harry moved to D.C. after the election.

Yes, very soon, this life would be theirs permanently, and nothing was going to get in the way.

PART FOUR

Friday, September 26
Day of the Murder

CHAPTER 18
NOEWARE, GA., OUTSIDE G.R.I.T. DEPOT

Even the chirping of the birds outside seemed dry and labored on this hot fall morning. The ground between the blades of grass cracked as if it belonged to some sandless desert landscape, seeming to allow a view straight to the Earth's molten core. Allison hadn't witnessed a lone sprinkle of rain since arriving in South Georgia, let alone a soaking downpour, which the wilting foliage certainly needed. Even Central America has a rainy season she thought, as she wandered around the still mostly empty downtown, drinking what almost passed as coffee that she had purchased at the Mean Bean coffee house just outside of the Grand Hotel. She winced at the bitterness of the brew, as she noticed a familiar face taking a respite on a bench.

Miss Willa had eyes of wonder this early morning. She appeared to be talking to the herd of gathering squirrels near her battered shoes, still holding her worn out Bible, and seeming to have not a care in the world. Allison stared at the older woman, again awed by everything that she had heard about her: tragic, she lives at the Grand Hotel, she's a nut. What is your story, Miss Willa, Allison asked herself for the hundredth time since her arrival in Noeware. She cautiously approached the bench, quietly clearing her throat in hopes of not startling the old woman and took a seat.

"Well, good morning, girl," Miss Willa said cheerfully, glancing in Allison's general direction, but not making eye contact. "We will have rain soon; the critters always know."

"Wouldn't that be nice," Allison asked looking skeptically up at the cloudless sky. "Do you have big plans for the day Miss Willa?"

"Oh, my yes, I am going on a great adventure."

"Going by train, I imagine?"

"I always travel by train, girl," the woman replied while waving to a gray-haired man standing just inside the train depot.

"Is that man painting?" Allison asked, not quite believing what she was seeing.

"Well, what else would he be doing? I don't suppose you've met R.W., yet?"

"I'm afraid that I haven't had the pleasure, but I'd sure like to."

Allison stretched her legs but remained seated on the bench. Her thoughts drifted to Atlanta and how a weekday's hustle and bustle would have begun hours earlier than the current time, in the metro area. She wasn't sure that she had been completely aware of how frenzied city life was, until she removed herself from it for a short time. She had attempted to call Jess this morning, after she had taken a shower, knowing that she wouldn't be waking her on a workday. Unfortunately, she had gotten voicemail — again. All Allison wanted was to recapture the excitement that had been so present in the first year of her relationship with Jess. She sighed, realizing that a mundane routine was what all relationships eventually evolved into. It didn't help that Jess spent more time in Indianapolis these days than she did in Atlanta. The alone time was great for Allison's studying, but it wreaked havoc on her love life. Something had to give. She made a mental note to discuss this with Jess when she returned to the city the next week.

Allison was shaken back to reality as the sounds of Miss Willa's mumbling trance appeared again. Just like the day that she had arrived in Noeware, Allison watched as Miss Willa stared into some unknown abyss, mumbling something almost silently under her breath. This time, because she had been expecting this exact thing to happen, Allison moved her face a bit closer to the woman, in hopes of catching a word or two. A word was exactly what she caught, a single word repeated over and over. Allison may not have answers, but perhaps she finally had a clue as to who this delightful woman had been, and what her story might be.

Miss Willa looked at Allison and smiled, returning to the present moment.

"I don't mean to be rude, my dear, but it is a little hot for such close contact."

Allison was red-faced, not having realized how closely she had moved in the woman's direction in order to hear her words. "You are absolutely right, Miss Willa. In fact, I think I am going to leave you alone and introduce myself to your friend. Did you say his name was R.W.?"

"Oh yes, go say hello. Don't be too long though, he and I have a trip to take."

THE HOPE OF A BLAST OF COOL AIR QUICKLY DISSIPATED, as Allison entered the train depot. There appeared to be just one antiquated air unit in a far window. Apparently, central air-conditioning had not been made a priority in the little town's budget, but then Allison expected that not a lot of folks waited for long periods of time on a train that simply circles the county.

"Good morning, Ms. Edwards, I've been looking forward to making your acquaintance," the gentleman said as he added brushstrokes to his canvas.

"I suppose at some point I'll get used to everyone already knowing who I am before I meet them," Allison replied while looking around for a trash receptacle to deposit the cup of swill disguised as coffee.

"They call me R.W., and I am happier than a drunk on a bender to meet you."

Smiling, Allison replied, "Likewise, R.W. Do you mind if I ask what you're painting? Oh, and please call me Allison."

"Just what I see, Allison, just what I see."

"I see."

"Do you? I've been observing the folks in this town for more years than I care to admit, and there ain't been a single one who seems to see things too clearly. But, if you are the first, may I offer my congratulations."

"I didn't mean to sound so self-assured, my apologies."

Smiling at her and nodding towards the purring orange tabby at her feet, R.W. added, "It looks like someone likes you."

"Good morning, Dewie," Allison said bending to rub behind the cat's ear. "She sure gets around, doesn't she?"

"That she does. She's a people person, umm, cat."

Allison sat down in a nearby chair, watching the man paint. His gray mullet put her more in mind of a car mechanic or a machinist, rather than an artist. Then again, he was a train engineer, right?

"How long do you plan to bless us with your presence here in town?"

"That's a very good question, R.W. I'm due to return to Atlanta next week, but I sure have a lot of interviews to complete in the meantime. Would you mind if I asked you a few questions, being that you're an observer and all?"

"Ask away, I'll try to help if I can."

"Do you mind if I ask you about Miss Willa?"

"What exactly would you like to know about the ole gal?"

"Anything, really. I am so drawn to her, for reasons that I can't explain."

"Well, let me ask you this, Allison, are you really drawn to Willa, or are you looking for anything else to occupy your mind, except focusing on your own troubles? You've been all over this county, talking to some important folks. You've learned some history, gotten the gossip, even met the mayor, but you are narrowing your thoughts to an unfortunate old lady."

Blushing, for what seemed like the third time already this morning, Allison replied, "I don't mean to be disrespectful at all. I'm sorry if I came across that way."

"Oh, I know you aren't trying to be disrespectful. I'm just saying, a snake spends his time climbing a porch rail in order to get to the eggs in a bird's nest, only to find the daddy bird is there and he's mad as a hornet. That snake thought he was in for a bluebird omelet, but what he got was his head pecked about half to death. But I digress …"

"What I hear you saying is that I should be careful what questions I ask, because I might not like the answers I receive."

"Is that what you hear me sayin'? Okay."

"Is that not what you meant?"

"Who am I to give advice to you, hell, we just met, right?"

Dewie hopped into Allisons lap and rubbed against her chest, purring ever so loudly, pacing back and forth. "Perhaps we did, but it doesn't feel so."

Smiling, R.W. briefly stopped painting and looked directly into Allison's eyes, "When a person seeks to know the truth about others, while escaping her own truth, it may be time for a change in direction."

Allison felt like she had been hit in the chest with a baseball bat. This man spoke to her as if he knew exactly who she was and what she was going through. "But I am writing a story about Noeware, I have to seek the truth."

"Noeware is a place, Allison, not a person, and it's certainly not the lady sitting out there on that bench."

He was absolutely right, Allison thought. She wasn't

brought here to write an expose' on a town's secrets, she was brought here to write a simple human-interest story. Soon, she would return to Atlanta, leaving everything and everyone in this town behind. Stirring the pot wasn't just the opposite of who she was, it was the opposite of what she was here to do. This conversation had definitely brought her some much-needed clarity.

"You've given me a lot to think about R.W., I sure appreciate it."

"Anytime, Allison. That's what I am here for, after all."

Patting Dewie on the head before placing her on a neighboring chair, Allison stood to leave. She had a lot on her plate today, but first she needed to check on Billy Washington. She exited the train depot, leaving the door to close with a soft thud. R.W. watched her leave, before glancing back at his painting. He signed the piece and gave it a once over. He had a sad look in his eyes as he stared at his work, a picture of Allison Edward's Atlanta apartment with a For Lease sign on its tiny front lawn.

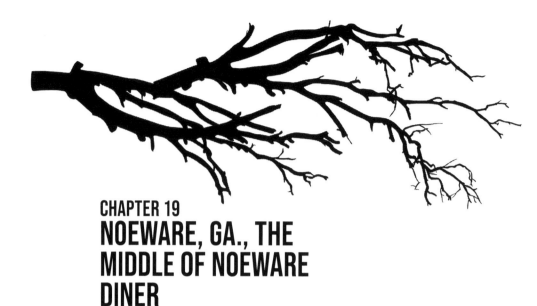

CHAPTER 19
NOEWARE, GA., THE MIDDLE OF NOEWARE DINER

"More coffee, Ruth?" Ned Wilson asked with a steaming pot in his hand. The regular crowd was apparently taking an extra few minutes to get out of bed this morning, as the diner was much slower than usual. He had already been here for hours cooking and prepping, but the mayor was the only customer sitting at the counter.

"Oh, go ahead Ned, I hardly slept a wink last night," Ruth replied with a yawn that she muffled with her hand.

The bell on the diner door chimed as Jeremiah Waddell entered, his muddy boots leaving residue on the immaculately clean checkered floor. He approached the counter with regret, not having considered that his nemesis might be here this morning.

Ned greeted him with a nod, while placing a cup of joe in front of his seat, which was two stools away from Ruth. "Now,

I don't want any trouble in here this morning, I expect everyone to behave themselves," Ned stated.

"I ain't going to hurt her; I just want some breakfast."

Ned replied with a laugh, "It wasn't YOUR temper I was worried about, Jeremiah."

Ruth glanced over in a disgust that was reserved for this particular man alone, eyeing the stump that served as his right hand, "I think I'll get a to-go cup for my coffee Ned, as hungry as I was, something has put me right off of the thought of food."

"Yes ma'am, give me just a sec."

"I expect you'll be home later this afternoon, Mr. Waddell? Chief Thomas wants to have a word or two with you."

"We've done talked to the police yesterday; this is harassment. Ernie Thomas don't have any reason to venture out to the county to talk to me about nothin'."

"On the contrary, Jeremiah, a crime was committed in his jurisdiction. Therefore, he has every right to collect a statement."

"You two need to take this outside," Ned said, returning with the mayor's paper cup.

"No need, I've said all that I intend to," Ruth offered as she took the cup from Ned's hand. Standing, she slid her walker over to help lift herself up. As she approached the door, Jeremiah Waddell ran in front of her to open it.

"I wouldn't want you to spill that coffee all over yourself and get burned, Ruth."

"I've been opening my own doors since I could walk, Mr. Waddell. The day I need help from the likes of you, is the day they call in hospice," Ruth offered as she reached around Jeremiah and grabbed the door handle.

Returning to the counter, Jeremiah mumbled under his breath, "Bitch."

"Ha, behind every bitch, Jeremiah, there's a woman with good reason," Ned replied, "I suspect you know exactly what her reasoning is."

As Ruth exited the diner, she caught a glimpse of Allison Edwards heading in the direction of the coffee house. She assumed that she was headed over to see William, who lived right above it. She'd noticed how close the two had become in a very short time, and she wondered what information Allison had offered him about her life back in Atlanta. Ruth knew that she had to be very careful with regards to the questions that she asked, but she was sure that William would share what he had learned, the word discretion was not in his vocabulary. She made a mental note to meet up with her nephew later.

Allison entered the building from behind, the entrance that was reserved for the residents of the two lofts above the coffee house, Billy Washington and Ruth Blakely. While she waited on the slow industrial elevator, she reflected on her conversation with R.W. Now, there's a man she wished she could take back to Atlanta with her. She just knew he could sort her life out in a hurry. His blunt advice had been exactly what she needed to hear this morning.

CHAPTER 20
NOEWARE, GA., BILLY WASHINGTON'S LOFT

Allison could hear a cat bellowing from her position outside of the loft door. Every step she took, every knock on the door, every meow from the cat seemed to echo off of the metal railings and concrete walls and floors. The dim lighting put her in mind of an emergency stairwell that could be found in almost any commercial building. This was the type of residence that she would have expected to see in Midtown Atlanta, not in a tiny South Georgia town. She found it comforting.

Throwing the door open with flourish, Billy Washington greeted her with a rehearsed smile that she knew he had plastered on to hide his current pain level.

"G.H., welcome to my humble abode."

"You should be resting; the last few days haven't been very good to you."

"There will be time to rest when I'm dead, my lady, and

despite the attempts of some nasty skinhead, that won't be in the immediate future."

Shaking her head, Allison led Billy back to the spot on the sofa that appeared to have been his perch prior to her arrival. Taking in her surroundings, she appreciated her new friend's attempt to soften up the urban space. Hot pink and bright yellow curtains in vibrant abstract patterns adorned the exceptionally tall factory windows. Framed panels of fabric in primary colors were used to sporadically decorate the walls. A black and red area rug covered most of the sealed concrete floor and lay under a canary yellow sofa with black throw pillows.

"I love what you've done with this space, Billy, it's really cheerful."

"Oh, you like it? I call it whorehouse chic," he replied with a giggle.

Returning his laugh, Allison sat down and scanned the room for the culprit responsible for the meowing. "Is Dewie in here? I thought you said she never meowed."

"Dewie? Lawd no, G.H., that's MY girl making all that noise. She'll likely not come out to greet you. She rarely makes an appearance, which is why I call her 'Garbo'. She is a gorgeous blue-eyed Siamese that I rescued a few years ago. You'll have to take my word on the gorgeous part, as she's a bit old and set in her ways."

"You rescued a senior cat? That's fantastic!"

"Well, don't give me too much credit. I was looking at an adorable Persian-mix at the pound, and Miss Thing started squawking and wouldn't take no for an answer. I guess she figured she had been in a cage long enough and didn't intend to stay in one a minute longer."

The story told Allison a lot about this man's character. She had always thought that you could tell a lot about a person by the way that he/she treated animals. Tucking her leg under her body as she sat sideways facing Billy, Allison reluctantly asked the obvious question, "so, any idea who the guy was that attacked you?"

Wincing a little, as he turned to face her as well, Billy replied, "I've been thinking a lot about that. I honestly don't think that I have ever seen him before. I just don't see any way that I could see a skinhead hanging around town and not remember it."

"Fair enough," Allison said nodding in agreement, sure that she would remember seeing such a person, herself.

"If you don't mind, I would sure rather talk about something more upbeat. What is on your agenda for this beautiful day?"

"Well, I have some free time this afternoon, but I thought I would try to see if I can swing an interview with Harrison Tennyson."

"Ohhhhhh, get you lady, hobnobbing with the upper crust."

"The keyword in that sentence was 'try'; I don't have a thing scheduled yet. Though, I think I've made friends with his daughters. I'm hoping they'll call in a bit of a favor."

"Ohhhhhh," Billy squealed, "I looooove me some Gail and Meg! That Gail is so sweet, just like that Hope on *Days of Our Lives* and Meg is so … blunt."

"Yes, I had a similar impression of them."

"Well, I have a proposition for you. Why don't you do what you need to do this afternoon and meet me back here around dinnertime? I'll call in an order to Ned, and you can pick it up from the diner on the way, my treat. I have quite the collection of chick flicks on dvd, we can have a movie night. I'll even do your hair."

"Chick Flicks? Honestly, you really are determined to get me riled up," she replied with a smile. "Actually, I think that sounds pretty perfect, but I insist on paying."

"But I'm the man," he teased, batting his eyes.

"Oh, dear God."

CHAPTER 21
NOEWARE, GA., MEAN BEAN COFFEE

The central air was no match for the Georgia heat, sweat dripped down from Cash Waddell's black mullet as he waited for his coffee to arrive on the counter. This establishment was not a frequent stop of his, but Ruth Blakely was standing outside of the diner when he passed, and he wasn't eager to risk round two with her this week. His name was called just in time for him to grab his drink and walk outside to answer the ringing phone in his pocket.

"Yeah," he said after hitting the answer button. "Huh? What problem? A concerned look took over his already grimaced face. "I don't know that that is going to work, he was only hired for the one job." Looking around to be sure that he was not being overheard and using his forearm to wipe the perspiration from his brow, he listened to the caller. "Alright, let me see what I can do. It's not going to be easy to convince him, with him knowing that the police have a description and all, but we'll see." He sat down on a nearby bench, almost in disbelief that he was hearing what he was hearing. Finally, the directions stopped long enough for him to get a word in, "I see. I'll take care of it. Just leave it to me, I'll make it happen."

Disconnecting the call, Cash took a minute to process the information. This was not part of the plan at all. There was one job that the nazi was recruited for. That job had been completed, though in a sloppy manner. He would be expecting payment so that he could get out of Tennyson County as quickly as possible. Now, he had to make the guy an offer that he couldn't refuse, with an even higher payout, and the new plan had to happen tonight. What had he gotten himself into?

He took a few minutes to ponder all this new information. Deciding on a course of action, he stood up and walked over to the door of the Grand Hotel.

BEHIND THE FRONT DESK OF THE HOTEL, DAISY WEI HAD just completed the check-in procedure for a guest when she caught a glimpse of Cash Waddell walking into the lobby. Trying not to be obvious with her stare, she quickly looked back at her computer screen. She acted as if she hadn't noticed him when he appeared directly in front of her.

"Daisy, is Claire around here somewhere," he asked without a smidgen of small talk.

She looked up from the screen and hoped that she seemed

surprised that he was standing there, "She was on the far side of the lobby on her cell just a few minutes ago. Want me to see if I can call her?"

At that moment, Cash saw Claire and walked briskly in her direction without another word to Daisy, who was left to admire the view of him walking away.

Reaching Claire in a quiet corner, Cash said, "Look, we need to talk."

"I've told you not to come in here like this, someone is going to see us."

"There are some things that we don't need to discuss on a phone."

"I agree. Meet me on the back patio of the hotel in about five minutes."

Cash nodded and headed back out the front door of the hotel. If this was going to go down, it was going to be discussed thoroughly, not in a quick phone call. He had a lot to lose, and so did Claire Montgomery. It was important to get this right, there was zero room for error.

CHAPTER 22
TENNYSON COUNTY, TENNYSON RESIDENCE

Having heard the car approaching the outside, Harrison Tennyson opened his front door before the bell could be rung. He greeted his daughter Gail with a hug and Allison Edwards with a firm handshake, inviting them in out of the midday heat. Gail had run into Allison at the diner while both women were having lunch separately and offered to make a meeting with her father happen. Realizing that she had a light schedule for the afternoon, Gail had offered to drive Allison to her father's house.

Harrison led the ladies into his study, offering Allison a cocktail, while pouring a glass of water for his daughter. Refusing the alcohol, but agreeing to water herself, Allison pulled out a note pad and pen and prepared herself for a quick interview. Harrison had been honest on the phone, he was happy to talk to Allison, but he had somewhere to be in a few hours. Making themselves comfortable on the luxurious camel colored leather furniture, Harrison in a chair, Gail and Allison on the sofa, they got down to business.

"I really appreciate your time Mr. Tennyson; I know that you are a busy man with important things going on."

With a laugh, he said, "Busy, yes. Important things going on? That's debatable." Looking at the screen of his phone, seeing two missed calls from Congressman McDonald, Harrison offered his complete attention to Allison.

"Regardless, I don't want to take up too much of your time."

With a wave of his hand meant to brush off the suggestion that he didn't have time for this interview, Harrison replied, "What may I help you with, Ms. Edwards?"

"Well, I met with Mayor Blakely in order to get a feel for the city of Noeware, and to learn a little about its history. She was kind enough to enlighten me on a little county history as well. I'd like to ask you some specifics."

"Ruth gave you background on the county's history, and she was kind? Are you sure that you met with Ruth Blakely? He smiled, knowing that the mayor would not bother holding back on her version of his family's history.

Gail Wilson quickly jumped into the conversation, "Now daddy, this interview is meant to be included in a human-interest piece for the paper, not a gossip column. This isn't the time or place for you to air out any dirty laundry about Mayor Blakely."

Holding both hands up in surrender, Harrison replied, "You are absolutely right, my dear, I just hope that the mayor showed us the same courtesy."

Now focusing on Allison, Gail said, "Daddy and Mayor Blakely have a long and complicated history, Allison. You will find that this is the case with a lot of old families in small towns. I'm sure that daddy doesn't mean to give the impression that there is bad blood between the two of them."

"Gail, I can speak for myself, but I appreciate what you are trying to do." Now looking at Allison, Harrison continued, "My relationship with Ruth is very complicated, and goes back to childhood. Things were quite different around these parts back then, and so were Ruth and me. Ruth was an acquaintance of my older sister, Olivia, who unfortunately went missing without a trace back in the early 70s. Ruth wasn't exactly a fan of the way my parents went about searching for my sister, and my family wasn't exactly in Ruth Blakely's fan club due to her frankness on the matter."

"My goodness, I had no idea. I am so sorry to hear this. Mayor Blakely never mentioned a word about a missing person, nor the fact that you had an older sister."

"Well, she wouldn't have. Ruth took the situation very personally, only the lord knows why, and it isn't something that she prefers to talk about these days. It would have been easier if she had shown the same discretion back then."

As the interview continued, Allison thought back to her conversation with R.W. She'd recommitted herself to writing about Noeware itself rather than its denizens. But the people she spoke with made it difficult. Even the town elders, couldn't help but turn to the personal lives of other Noewarians at the slightest prompt. Keeping them on the topic of Noeware in the present day and age was a challenge. While Allison loved the authenticity, she wasn't sure that she was receiving a lot of useful information for her story. She was beginning to feel like there was an intriguing book to be written about these families, but that was not why she had been brought here. At least, she didn't THINK that was why she had been brought here.

As Gail Wilson's car made its way down the Tennyson driveway and out onto the main road, the two women rode briefly in silence. Gail wondered what the effect of her father's stories would have on the overall direction of Allison's article. Her Aunt Olivia, whom Gail had never met, was not a topic of conversation that her daddy usually entertained. It was highly unusual for him to talk about it at all. In fact, he preferred that no one in the family talk about it. Then, there was his openness about the tension between himself and Ruth Blakely. Why was this man, who was normally so deliberate and cautious in his speech, so frank with a reporter? None of this was typical.

Allison broke the silence first, "Neither you nor Meg mentioned your aunt's disappearance the other night. I was really taken aback when I heard the story. I want you to know that you can trust me. I would never say or write anything that would intentionally hurt you or your family."

"I truly believe you when you say that Allison. I don't think it was intentional on my part, nor Meg's, to hold something that big back. You must understand, we don't really talk about Aunt Olivia's disappearance. It happened long before Meg and I were born, and it is terribly painful still for daddy and Aunt Claire."

"That must have been the story of the decade in a town this small, especially back in the 1970s."

"More like the story of the century! The way I understand it, the media from Florida to Virginia covered it nonstop, until the next big story happened."

"I don't doubt that. A girl from a wealthy and prominent family goes missing, that's a huge deal."

"It sure is. The sad part is, Aunt Olivia was the second child that disappeared from Tennyson County around that time period. The first girl wasn't from a family that excited the newshounds as much. They pretty much chalked her disappearance up to teenage angst and assumed she had run away from home."

"How do they know she didn't?"

"I don't know that anyone knows for sure, but she returned home almost 25 years later. Do runaways return home after nearly two and a half decades of being gone?"

"That's a good point. What kind of story did she offer as to what might have happened?"

"That's the most unfortunate part, the woman has severe dementia. She couldn't offer any type of explanation."

"The poor woman. I wonder how she even knew where home was."

"Another good question. The whole thing is tragic. The disappearance of Olivia Tennyson was Headline News, almost no one, outside of Tennyson County that is, even remembers the disappearance of Wilhelmina Banks."

"Wilhelmina Banks? That is her name?"

"That WAS her name. These days no one is quite so formal. To all of us, she is just Miss Willa.

CHAPTER 23
NOEWARE, GA., MIDDLE OF NOEWARE DINER

The lunch rush had passed hours ago, and he had at least an hour before the regulars started coming in for dinner, so Ned Wilson took advantage of some well-earned downtime by joining Gail in the corner booth she occupied. Sitting across from her, he placed two fresh cups of coffee on the table, "penny for your thoughts."

Snapping back to reality, Gail focused her attention on the man. She took in his kind blue eyes, eyes that she never got tired of staring into. She noticed that his crow's feet were becoming a little more pronounced, like mini sand dunes spreading like English ivy in a formal garden. Wrinkles around the corners of his mouth showed more than his age, they were a testament to the wisdom that this lovely man had gained over a lifetime of hard work and experience. He had earned every gray hair on his head, by never taking the easiest road, but always following his own path. He looked like he had lost a few pounds, this worried Gail. Was he eating? Getting enough sleep?

The truth was none of this was any of her business anymore. She had seen to that. Self-doubt and over protection had led her to dissolve the marriage to the only man that she had ever loved. When they had met, she saw stars, like a heroine in some fairytale. Those stars shown more brightly year after year, and to this day, twinkled every single time she saw him. A herd of butterflies took up residence in her stomach with the mere thought of Ned Wilson. She saw no need to change her last name after their divorce was final, he was her man, always would be, even if life's circumstances wouldn't allow them to be together.

"Earth to Gail," he said, clearing his throat in a grasp for attention.

"I'm sorry, I am a million miles away."

"Everything okay?"

"Why are you so kind to me?"

Covering both of her hands in the center of the table with both of his own, he smiled before answering, "it's you, my dear, who is the queen of kindness, even if it's a little misguided."

"Let's not go over all of that again, I have had a very emotional afternoon."

"Want to tell me about it?"

"I want to tell you everything about it, but want to say nothing about it, too."

"Just enjoy your coffee, we don't have to talk."

This was the way she always knew that this man was perfect for her. They could talk about anything, absolutely anything, but they were both completely comfortable in their collective silence as well. In fact, sometimes when they were quiet, they spoke volumes to each other. She could feel, with every fiber of her being, how much love he had for her. She also knew that he would take her back tomorrow if she only gave the word. That fact was exactly why it was so dangerous for her to spend time with him alone. A million times a week, she had to stop herself from begging for forgiveness, an apology he assured her she did not owe, and returning to their marriage — where she belonged.

NO! She did not belong in that marriage. Her emotions and actions were volatile. She could be a clone of Donna Reed one minute, the perfect wife, and the daughter of Satan the next. But wasn't that just due to the alcohol? Hadn't she been sober for years at this point? The answer was yes and no. Dry she was, as in without alcohol, but was she sober? Had she gotten far enough in recovery to forgive herself for the things that she had put this caring man through? Afterall, an addict's sobriety started anew every 24 hours. One day at a time she stayed dry, one day at a time she tried not to hurt Ned Wilson. Yet, she could see the ache in his heart every time he looked at her.

Ned didn't sign up to be the husband of a raging alcoholic. The truth is, Gail barely drank on New Year's Eve when they first dated. Things had changed when he bought the diner from Polly Carter, and she took the management job at the hotel. Long hours apart, stressful workdays, and endless life demands had morphed her into someone she didn't recognize. Someone that her husband didn't recognize. Someone her friends and colleagues didn't recognize.

She was lying to herself again. Yes, all these pressures had contributed to her alcoholism, but they weren't the catalyst. Denial was ever-present in her mind. It was so much easier to blame herself and the life that she had chosen, than admit the reason her drinking truly spiraled out of control. It just wasn't in her nature to blame others for her shortfalls. But was this blame a bad thing, if it was true? Was it true, or had she just convinced herself that it was? In her heart, she knew the answer to that question, and she would never be able to move on with her life until she accepted this reality, and confronted the evil that she knew existed. Until then, one day at a time.

GAIL HAD SPENT ANOTHER HOUR AT THE DINER, BEFORE she headed home to get some rest. Ned knew that something was weighing heavy on his ex-wife, and it killed him that there was nothing that he could do about it. When would she forgive herself for that fateful night? He had forgiven her almost immediately. He reluctantly accepted her divorce decision, knowing that nothing could come before her sobriety, but that was years ago now. He wasn't losing patience with her, as he would wait an eternity for Gail Wilson, but he was aware of his own mortality, and it killed him to know that so much time was being wasted — time that they should have been sharing their lives.

The bell on the door rang as Allison Edwards exited with her takeout order. Cash Waddell had been in and out grabbing coffee. Ruth Blakely called in a salad order to take home for dinner. Ned was vaguely aware of any of this, though he had participated in every transaction. He was a shell of himself, just an empty vessel longing to reconnect with the love of his life. He wanted to grab her, shake her, make her understand what she was losing — what they were losing. He also knew that the decision was up to her. For now, like he had done every night for years, he'd sleep in the knowledge that all was not lost, just paused. He had to believe that, as the alternative was unbearable.

Her beautiful smile. Her perfectly manicured nails. Her nurturing heart. Her smooth skin. Was she aware at all that she was killing him with every second they were apart? That what happened that night, as awful as it was, paled in comparison to what she was doing to him now? He had to hold on to the hope, no, the belief, that one day they would be together again, and live the closest to happily ever after possible. Then, and only then, HE would have the opportunity to make a confession and ask for forgiveness. Would she be as ready to accept his apology? He could only pray that she would. Although a confession of his own might make it easier for Gail to forgive herself, she could easily hate him for keeping a secret of his own. Not to mention, it wasn't just his secret, Ruth might have something to say about him telling this truth.

CHAPTER 24
NOEWARE, GA., BILLY WASHINGTON'S LOFT

"It's open," Billy yelled from his place on the sofa after Allison's first knock. His rib injuries were too painful to get up again once he was settled. He was dressed in navy blue and white pin-striped pajamas with matching blue fuzzy slippers, TV remote in hand. With a guilty grin, he greeted his friend, "Ready to Netflix and chill?"

"You are impossible, you know that?"

"I do know that, G.H., self-awareness is my superpower."

Shaking her head, but finding it hard not to return his smile, Allison set their dinner on the coffee table. She removed the food containers from their bag and walked to the kitchen to find some utensils. The place was immaculate. "Ummm-mmm, you should be resting, not cleaning. You could eat off of these floors."

"If it's all the same to you, I'd prefer you grab us a couple of plates from that lefthand cabinet. For the record, I have been resting, Auntie sent her cleaning lady over to freshen the place up."

"That was certainly nice of Ruth, she sure takes good care of you."

"I have many guardian angels, G.H., Auntie Ruth is just one of a long line."

Allison believed this to be true. She only wished that she was as close to her family as Billy was to his family. She was also thankful that Miss Willa, another guardian angel, entered the ally when she did the other night. If she hadn't, things may have turned out a whole lot different for Billy Washington.

"Alright G.H., spill ... I want to know every torrid detail of your meeting at Tennyson Place this afternoon. You may start with the décor, was it tacky? Tell me it was tacky."

Laughing, Allison replied, "Sorry to disappoint you, but it was very tastefully furnished. In fact, I am pretty sure that the sofa in Harrison Tennyson's study cost more than everything that I own."

"Damn it," Billy replied shaking his head, taste AND money, bitches."

"Are we going to eat, or are we going to gossip about the Tennyson family all evening?"

"Why not both?" Billy responded while transferring grilled cheese sandwiches and fries onto the plates Allison had brought from the kitchen."

About four episodes into the period drama that Billy had chosen for them to watch, and long after they had polished off the food, the two had dozed off. The show may be a hit with streaming viewers, but it didn't appear to hold their attention. Billy was exhausted from the goings on of the past few days, and Allison had worn herself out interviewing the people of South Georgia and sleeping in a strange bed. The sofa was just comfortable enough to lull them both into slumber.

MMMEEEOOOWWW …

Like an alarm clock, Garbo's caterwaul shot them both to attention. She had pranced in from the bedroom, where she had obviously been asleep for a few hours. Well, her nap was over, and she made sure that everyone else was up too, to shower her with adoration. She jumped up on the sofa between them and took turns rubbing her head from one to the other.

"What the hell was that?" Billy asked, wiping sleep from his eyes.

"Don't you recognize the screams of your own cat? I mean, she's right here, Billy."

"Not THAT noise, G.H., the one outside. You don't hear those sirens?"

Allison had spent her entire life living within the city limits of Atlanta. One learns to tune out traffic and siren noise when they are constant. In fact, Allison had heard the sirens, mostly subconsciously, but in the city that's just the sound-track of daily life. Now that it was a topic of conversation, she had to admit that this seemed off. This might even be the first siren sound that she had heard since she had arrived, and there were several of them.

They were both wide awake now and headed for the windows, Billy's curiosity so peaked, he forgot all about his earlier pain. Opening the blinds for them, Billy moved next to Allison overlooking the street below. They looked at each other in shock as they saw multiple ambulances and police squad cars in front of the Grand Hotel, Billy's shock from wonder about what was going on, Allison's shock from curiosity over why ambulances would be used when the hospital was practically next door.

Allison spoke first, "I am going down to see what the hell is going on."

"Not without me you aren't," Billy exclaimed while looking around for his door keys.

"You are staying here. You have been through enough in the past few days. I promise you I will text the second I know something. Besides, I have an excuse to be down there, I'm a guest at the hotel."

Reluctantly, Billy agreed that she was right. It was against his very nature not to run down to that street and get in the middle of the action, but the realization that his pain was returning led him back to the sofa.

"You will text me the second you know something?"

"The very second, I promise," Allison said as she headed out the door.

"I want every tiny detail," Billy yelled at the already closing door.

Allison had only made it two steps outside of the loft building when the storm hit. The rain was extraordinary in its ferociousness. Without an umbrella, she ran back to the door and stepped inside. Waiting out the storm seemed reasonable, as rain was already flooding the street behind the buildings. The few seconds that she was outside left her soaked to the bone. She sat on the bottom step and tried to be patient, hoping that this was one of those brief summer storms that would disappear as quickly as it came.

CHAPTER 25
NOEWARE, GA., GRAND HOTEL

Chief Ernie Thomas caught up with Claire Montgomery at the front desk. He had sent a uniformed officer down to instruct her to queue up the security footage for the evening. True to form, she had given the officer a tongue-lashing for assuming that she hadn't been intelligent enough to think of that already. Now, the chief joined Claire in her office to review the video.

"Ruth has already called to find out what's going on. The rain has saved us for a few minutes, as she'd have a hard time navigating a walker while holding an umbrella," Ernie Thomas said.

"Well, it's not like there is anything that she could do anyway, every one of your officers is here, but I know that won't stop her from coming over to tell us all how poorly we are handling the situation."

Chief Thomas pulled a chair up beside the desk chair that Claire was already sitting in. Side by side, they stared at the computer monitor as Claire started the footage. They both had the same thought; this was going to be a very long night.

While the video played, Chief Thomas took the opportunity to question Claire a little.

"Remind me why the fourth floor is unoccupied?"

"We were in the process of wallpapering the walls, it hasn't been done in years. I suppose we are lucky that this happened before we finished the job, though now the carpet will have to be changed, too."

"Jesus Claire, you are a cold fish, aren't you?"

"I don't mean to come across that way, Ernie. I have been a realist my entire life." When their sister had gone missing, Claire couldn't help but feel lost in the drama. She had the distinct impression that everyone around her, including her parents (and perhaps especially Camille) were feeding into the drama. Harry had been so emotional, leaving Claire to be the rock. "It's not that I don't feel things, I am just a problem-solver. I'm always thinking of the next thing that must be done. It's a trait that makes me ideal to manage this hotel."

"Fair enough. Now, tell me why Ms. …"

Before Chief Thomas could finish his thought, he received a call from one of his officers assigned to the fourth floor. Gail Wilson had been located and was currently being attended to by emergency medical technicians. The chief thanked the officer and dropped the call.

"They located Gail. She was unconscious upstairs. EMTs are looking at her now, but she appears to be okay."

"Unconscious? Where the hell was she?"

"It appears that she was at the end of the hall, in the closet."

"In the closet? Well, that's par for the course in this town," Claire replied standing with the intention of heading up to check on her niece.

"You can just sit back down Claire. You won't get past my officers on the fourth floor. Let's just keep reviewing footage, not that I expect we'll see much."

"Why do you say that Ernie?"

"The security camera on the fourth floor had been turned to aim at the ceiling. I would recommend you either move the security cameras so that they are not installed directly above supply closets containing mops and brooms with handles long enough to be used to tilt said cameras or lock the damn closet doors."

"You really must think me a fool, Ernie. Those doors are always locked."

"I see. While we watch this video, wanna tell me why someone was allowed to enter a room on the fourth floor?"

"I'd love to tell you, but I have no idea. My guess is Gail will be able to tell us when she comes down."

GAIL WILSON MADE HER WAY INTO THE DESERTED HOTEL lobby. All the police, medical, and hotel workers were either on the fourth floor or were outside. Gail was extremely nauseated, and her chest and nasal passages were burning from the chemical used to render her unconscious. With every breath, she offered a raspy cough, but the EMTs that tended to her agreed that she would be okay. She entered Claire Montgomery's office without knocking, as the door was open per police protocol that dictated a male and female not be alone behind a closed door. Claire paused the video footage as she noticed Gail's entrance. Standing, she walked over and took Gail in her arms.

Pulling back and looking over Gail's face, Claire asked, "Are you okay? What in the world happened up there?"

"That's exactly what I want to know," Ernie Thomas added.

Gail explained the series of events as best she could, still being a little foggy from the inhalant, and being very emotional from the evening's events.

She had just arrived at work, for a shift that she had not planned on working, as Daisy Wei had taken ill and couldn't come in. A woman had approached the desk with a situation that she hoped Gail could help her with. She wished to surprise her significant other with dinner, but her other half did not know that she was in town. Again, it was a surprise. The woman wanted to know if she could freshen up in a room, before the surprise. Gail didn't think it would be an issue to let the woman freshen up in an unused room on the fourth floor. She led the woman to the room, opened the door for her, but couldn't remember much of anything after the door closed. She assumes that she was grabbed from behind by someone and left in the supply closet while the murder took place.

Gail fell into uncontrollable sobs when she finished her recollection of what happened.

Between deep breaths, trying to prevent herself from

hyperventilating, she asked, "has anyone told Allison Edwards what happened?"

"Allison Edwards, what does that journalist have to do with any of this?" Claire Montgomery asked.

"Damn it, are you telling me that Jessica Walters is Allison Edwards' lover?" Chief Thomas responded after making the connection.

"Yes, she is," Gail replied.

"This just gets better and better," the man said while shaking his head.

"What gets better and better, Chief Thomas?" Mayor Ruth Blakely asked as she entered the door to the office.

OUTSIDE THE HOTEL, THE RAIN HAD ENDED. STEAM WAS rising from the hot streets, that were now mostly empty as the spectators dispersed during the storm. Allison Edwards stood beside a few police officers who were still maintaining a police line. She looked around at the sound of her name being called and saw Gail Wilson approaching her. Under the streetlights, even from a distance, it was obvious that Gail Wilson had been crying. The woman's eyes were puffy, her nose and upper lip red from wiping them with tissue. She approached Allison with a resigned look on her face.

"Allison, let's go over here and sit down for a minute, okay?"

"Gail, what's going on?" Allison asked, suddenly finding it difficult to breathe.

"Allison, it's Jessica…"

Gail didn't finish her sentence before Allison vomited on the pavement between them. She didn't need to hear Gail say it, she knew. It was just like Jess to drive down and surprise her, and this explained why Allison had been unable to reach her by phone over the last 24 hours.

"Allison, come sit over here with me," Gail pleaded, leading Allison to a nearby bench.

Voice shaking, eyes showing signs of shock, Allison asked, "Is she dead?"

In a near whisper, Gail reluctantly replied, "I'm afraid so, sweetheart. I'm so sorry."

CHAPTER 26
FOOD FOR THOUGHT

Tennyson County, Washington Resident

Alex knew it was going to be another long night. Anxiety had deprived him of sleep for days now. His homework assignments had been pushed off to the backburner and replaced with endless rounds of video games, to make himself available to RedDragn111. He was terrified of getting caught once he started selling the drugs but was thrilled at the prospect of finally becoming more than the weird kid with the gay uncle and absent parents. It all seemed like pointless worry, as he hadn't heard from his gaming buddy in a few days. Relax, he told himself, it may never happen. He was just about to sign off and go to bed for the evening when a message appeared onscreen:

RedDragn111: You there, my dude?

KidOutaNoeware2011: Yea

KidOutaNoeware2011: where ya been?

KidOutaNoeware2011: I thought you changed your mind.

RedDragn111: I had to get the pills man.

RedDragn111: You still up for an exchange?

KidOutaNoeware2011: Yup. When? Where?

RedDragn111: Tomorrow after 2.

RedDragn111: I'll leave them in a plastic grocery bag under some leaves behind Frog Rock.

KidOutaNoeware2011: Frog Rock?

KidOutaNoeware2011: Seriously?

RedDragn111: Yup

RedDragn111: Scenic Hwy

RedDragn111: out at the old drainage ditch

RedDragn111: know it?

KidOutaNoeware2011: Yea. I know it

> KidOutaNoeware2011: I'll grab them tomorrow.

Alex signed off the game for the evening, his stomach in knots. He knew exactly where Frog Rock was, and he was beginning to wonder what he was getting himself into.

Noeware, Ga., Grand Hotel

POLICE CHIEF ERNIE THOMAS WAS ON HIS THIRD CUP OF coffee, still going over security footage with hotel General Manager Claire Montgomery. The tension in the room was as thick as molasses. Claire was just about the last person in Tennyson County that Ernie would choose to spend hours with. He was just about to suggest that they take a quick break to stretch their legs when they both saw it at the same time.

Bolting straight up in her chair, Claire exclaimed, "This is it. Oh my God, there's Gail opening the door for the girl."

The footage showed Gail Wilson using her magnetic key to unlock the hotel room. She remained in the hall, holding the door open for Jessica Walters to enter with what appeared to be an overnight bag over her shoulder. She could be seen saying something to Jessica, but never entering the room. She then shut the door slowly and turned to head back toward the elevator. Pressing the down button, she waited, but not for long as a male figure, head shaved, approached from the direction of the supply closet. Startled, obviously seeing the assailant's reflection in the elevator door, Gail turned to face him. His cloth-filled hand covered her shocked expression for what appeared an eternity, Gail struggling the entire time.

As Gail Wilson lost consciousness, the man supported her by grabbing her under both arms, never allowing her to sink completely to the floor. With some effort, as he was slight, and deadweight is remarkably heavy, he drug her in the direction of the closet, returning within seconds to retrieve the keycard that Gail had dropped by the elevator. The card would be unnecessary, as the room door flew open, Jessica Walters obviously hearing the commotion in the otherwise silent hallway. Whether she said anything was unclear, as the footage did not include audio, but the man produced what appeared to be a hunting style knife from his black and gray camouflage fatigues and charged into the room, hitting her with the force of his hunched body, as if he was a professional football player on a field. She appeared to be a good six inches taller than the man.

"Who in the hell is that?" Claire asked, visibly shaken from watching her niece's run-in with a murderer.

"I'll be damned. I'll have to get some still pictures from the video to show Billy Washington, but if I had to guess, this is the skinhead that battered him the other evening," the chief replied, as they watched an open hotel room door and empty hallway for several minutes.

"You really think some random person attacked Billy Washington and stayed in town for a few days to kill a stranger from out of town?"

Glancing over at Claire with a skeptical look, Ernie

Thomas replied, "No Claire, I don't think this was random at all."

Suddenly, the killer exited the room, staggering in exhaustion, and headed back toward the supply closet. Ernie and Claire sat motionless, eyes glued to the screen, silent. A moment later, the screen went blank. They looked at each other, not immediately knowing what to say. Finally ...

"What just happened?" Claire asked, a look of total confusion in her eyes.

"Someone tilted the camera."

"Why would he move the camera after the fact? This doesn't make any sense."

"I don't think HE did," Chief Thomas replied. "I'd say that our killer is an idiot who never considered a security camera, but he had an accomplice that knew that it was there."

"Are you sure that you aren't jumping to conclusions, Ernie?"

"We'll have to see if the FBI agrees with me, Claire. It looks like we might have a federal hate crime on our hands."

"Hate crime?", Claire responded in astonishment. "You mean because Jessica was in a relationship with another woman? You think THAT was motive for murder? I find that highly unlikely."

"Oh no, I don't think her relationship in and of itself was a motive for murder, but I DO think that Ms. Walters being transgender may have played a role in what happened.

"Transgender!" Claire exclaimed seemingly shocked.

"I suspect that someone in Tennyson County knew this little tidbit of information, and he or she had a reason for not wanting this particular cat to get out of the bag."

Noeware, Ga., Outside of the Grand Hotel

Gail Wilson and Allison Edwards heard the commotion at the same time. A man was attempting to cross the police line and enter the hotel but was facing resistance from the uniform officers stationed to guard it. The man tried to physically force his way between two of the policemen, ducking to go under the yellow crime scene tape.

"Sir, no one is allowed to enter the hotel currently," one of the officers said as he pushed the man back.

"I've got to get in there."

"If you are a guest sir, you'll be allowed to go in and get your things just as soon as I get the word."

"You don't understand …"

"Enlighten me then."

"I'm looking for someone. She was in the hotel. I can't find her anywhere."

"What's her name, sir," the officer asked, trying to encourage the clearly agitated man to remain calm.

Allison and Gail, unable to concentrate on anything other than the current drama at hand, watched intently. The man sat on the wet pavement, weary from worry, beginning to sob.

"Jess, Jessica Walters."

The look on Allison's face changed immediately. What had been an expression of clear grief, became utter confusion. She stood from the bench and took a few steps closer to the now hyperventilating man. She reached him just in time for oxygen to return to his lungs.

"She's my wife," he said, as he completely broke down again, Allison Edwards fainting beside him.

Noeware, Ga., Outside the G.R.I.T. Depot

THE SUN WAS RISING SEVERAL HOURS AFTER MOST OF THE commotion at the hotel had subsided. There were still police and reporters everywhere, but guests had been allowed to collect their belongings, the body of the deceased had been removed by the coroner. Assurances were made that the hotel could reopen for business within 24 hours. The fourth floor would remain unavailable to guests and staff, as it was an active crime scene, but due to the remodeling, it was not in use anyway.

Miss Willa sat on a bench humming to herself. She appeared to be completely unfazed by the town's current drama. She was in her own little world, where she spent nearly all her time. The train would be firing up soon to start a long day's work and she thought that she might ride out to the county for a while. From a distance, she watched an approaching visitor, armed with a cup of coffee. Maneuvering a walker, while holding the hot cup, seemed to be second nature to the woman.

Reaching the bench, Mayor Ruth Blakely took a seat next

to Miss Willa, but continued to look straight ahead, rather than make eye contact. In fact, both women focused their gazes elsewhere. For a few minutes, they remained silent, taking in the rising sun, breathing the fresh air. Eventually, Miss Willa spoke, "that girl, the one at the hotel, she's dead?"

"She is," Ruth Blakely replied.

"Was it my little girl?"

"What? Oh God no, you silly old woman."

Ruth took a sip of her hot coffee, continuing her blank stare forward. Sitting her coffee cup down on the bench beside her, she removed her thick eyeglasses, huffed a little steam on them and wiped them with the tail of her blouse to clean them. This act was to no avail, as the humidity produced from the early morning storm would just fog them back up in seconds, but she needed to fidget away some of her pent-up nervous energy.

"Are you sure it wasn't my little girl, Ruthie?"

Using her walker to assist her in rising from the bench, Ruth grabbed her coffee and started back in the direction from which she had arrived. Over her shoulder, she answered Miss Willa, "I'm positive, my friend. I'm afraid it was MY little girl, and I might as well have killed her myself."

EPILOGUE

Tennyson County, Owens Creek, 1973

The afternoon was unseasonably cool as Ruth Blakely stared at the flowing water. Her thoughts carried her back to this very day one year ago, in this exact spot. What had started out as such a beautiful afternoon had ended in unbelievable heartache and confusion. Ruth asked the universe for the thousandth time, why those boys had to show up and ruin the closest moment to perfection she had ever known. She lost the better part of her soul that day and she couldn't foresee a day that she'd ever get over it. She looked at the object in her left hand with sadness, resignation in her eyes, the grief overpowering.

Too similar to that day a year ago, she heard the now foreboding sound of rustling leaves behind her. She quickly closed her left fist and grabbed her cane with her right one, intent on using it as a weapon this time. She raised it up baseball bat style and turned her body around to find a familiar face behind her. He had stopped at a respectable distance, obviously trying to avoid startling her.

"Don't you take another step Harrison Tennyson, I will beat you to death, that's for sure."

Holding both hands up in surrender, Harrison replied, "I thought I might find you here, Ruth. There's no need for the cane, I come in peace."

"Why are you looking for me?"

"Well, I figured that no one else on earth, besides the two of us, knows what today is. I haven't been able to concentrate on anything else today other than Olivia."

"Did you bring those boys with ya? Are you trying to finish what you started?"

"I was wrong Ruth. I got caught up in a moment. I've tried to apologize to you, but you won't talk to me."

"Do ya blame me? I had never seen anybody in my life so scared as I saw Olivia that day. Jeremiah chasing her through the woods heckling her like the opposing football team. That just wasn't right. You would have done anything to be seen as a cool kid, including allowing your own sister to be assaulted. You ought to be ashamed."

"More ashamed than you'll ever know, Ruth. I'd say that you and I both lost our best friend that day. It makes more sense for us to be here for each other, than for us to be sniping at each other like a couple of cocks in a fight."

"That's an interesting figure of speech, considering."

"Would you mind if I sit down? I promise you, I am alone and unarmed," he said, grinning for the first time.

"Do what you like," Ruth replied, finally lowering the cane.

"Well, is it true what they say, Ruth?"

"What exactly do they say, Harrison?"

"You know," he said while averting his eyes from her stare, "that you're a lezzy."

"I hear a lot of folks say you're an asshole, Harrison Tennyson, but I don't pay them any mind."

Laughing at her response, Harrison admitted, "that's probably because you know it's true."

"Maybe."

They both spent the next few minutes watching the creek water flow, enjoying the peace and quiet. Harrison glanced over at Ruth's tight left fist; she snuck a glance at the scar on his forehead. Still, they didn't say a word, just took a little time to try to become comfortable in each other's company. Not necessarily accomplishing the task.

Ruth spoke first, "I see your head healed up. You reckon you're gonna have a mark there for the rest of your life?"

"Maybe it'll go away one day, maybe it won't. I don't know. What I do know, is that you had every right to protect yourself from me that day."

"I never thought you were bad, Harrison Tennyson, but somebody had to knock some sense into you."

"You saved me from myself a year ago," Harrison said holding out his right palm to Ruth. "Maybe I was sent here today to do the same for you."

Ruth's gaze left his eyes and dropped to his open palm. Reluctantly, Ruth held her closed fist above his hand, opened it, and let the razor blade that she had taken from her mother's bathroom fall. A single drop of blood followed, where the blade had pierced her clinched fist. The symbolism of the moment was too much for Ruth. Tears began to flow down her dark cheeks, as every ounce of emotion that had built up for 12 months escaped from her eyes. Harrison responded by sliding in closer to Ruth and wrapping an arm around her shoulder.

"Promise me that you'll get out of this town and make something of yourself, Ruth Blakely," Harrison said as he used a hand to lift her chin, so that she met his stare. "Escaping Tennyson County AND making something of yourself, that'd be a twofer."

Immediately tense, Ruth spat back, "Don't you ever say that word to me again, not ever."

"Whoa now, I didn't mean anything by it. Just promise me, okay?"

"I promise," she replied, though the reality was that she had no way out of Tennyson County and was destined to spend a miserable life here for all her days. But, in that moment, she believed in the promise that she made.

Harrison, taken by the moment, kissed Ruth. To his surprise, she did nothing to discourage him, nor push him away. They were two teens in anguish, the only people in the world who could possibly understand what the other was feeling. Though they grieved separately, they shared a numbness that was easier to bear than the alternative.

"I'm never going to love you, Harrison Tennyson."

"I don't expect you'll even like me," he replied, kissing her again, while taking off his jacket, laying it on the ground behind her, and lowering her onto her back.

"I've felt nothing for so long. I just wanna feel something," Ruth said softly.

An unlikely alliance wasn't the only thing conceived that afternoon on the bank of Owen's Creek. It would only be a matter of months before Ruth Blake's promise to leave Tennyson County to better herself would become a reality. But on that day, as Ruth Blakely lay on her back, looking up at the autumn clouds, there was nothing between her and the heaven that Olivia had supposed for her, except Harrison Tennyson and a canopy of woven branches.

The Beginning…

COMING SOON BY G.L. YANCY

Woven Branches
Book 2
The Noeware Man

All characters and situations in this series are fictional. Any similarities between the characters/events and actual people/events, either living or deceased, are purely coincidental. I made this all up, y'all.

Independent authors live or die by your word of mouth and online reviews. If you enjoyed this novella, please consider leaving a review on Amazon, Goodreads, or wherever you normally review books.

To stay up to date on all things *Woven Branches*, please follow the "G. L. Yancy" and "Woven Branches" Facebook pages. You may also email your full name and email address to glyancybooks@outlook.com to join my mailing list. I will never spam you, only let you know when a new release is available.

I am forever grateful for the opportunity to entertain you … Please, be good to each other.

ACKNOWLEDGMENTS

Writing a book takes more than a village, it takes a small army …

I want to thank John Ross Branch, Jacob Perry, Tammy Bowen Wilkinson, Sgt. Chase Burnes, Louis Johnson, and Tiffany Bowerman PA-C for answering my technical, legal, and medical questions. Any facts that may be inaccurate stem from my misunderstanding, not from their lack of knowledge.

Thank you, Amy LeCroy Nichols, Jennifer LeCroy, and Tonya Sharp Freeman for sharing your childhood imaginations with me. Wow, we sure had some great times. Long live, **Three is More Than Enough.**

My eternal gratitude goes out to Tess Lake, author of the *Torrent Witch* series, and Lauretta Hannon, author of *The Cracker Queen*. The encouragement that you both have shown has warmed my heart. Folks, please buy their books.

Special thanks to Angie Occhipinti, Jennifer Kuzara, and Merritt Smith Croland for making this storyteller appear to be a writer. You three have made this a better book.

Thank you, Angelia Feathers, for the brilliant social media illustrations and Clara Stone at Authortree for the lovely cover design.

My heart belongs to R.H. Rankin, without whom this

series would not exist. You encouraged me to make my writing a priority, showed interest in my characters, asked a lot of questions (sometimes, too many questions) and allowed me to take my book seriously. I hope you are proud. I love you completely.

Lastly, to my dear readers … you have provided me the opportunity to fulfill a lifelong dream. When I was a little boy, I used to make paper dolls out of the thick catalogs that always arrived in the mail around the holidays. I was intrigued by the countless daytime and primetime soap operas that littered the TV schedules back then. I would use these dolls as characters in my little dramas and keep them hidden so that adults wouldn't think me odd. I wanted to grow up and create a soap opera of my own, though it never occurred to me that it would be in book form. To this day, I still use little dolls as placeholders when I am writing a chapter, to keep me focused on the scene that I am writing (YES, my Ruth doll uses a walker). Thank you all for allowing my characters to come out of hiding. I am eternally grateful.

Made in the USA
Columbia, SC
03 July 2024